The Spettecake Holiday

By Edith Unnerstad

THE SAUCEPAN JOURNEY
PYSEN
LITTLE O
THE SPETTECAKE HOLIDAY

The Spettecake Holiday

BY EDITH UNNERSTAD

Illustrated by Iben Clante

THE MACMILLAN COMPANY *New York*

Library of Congress catalog card number: 58–11081

Original title: FARMORSRESAN

Translated from the Swedish by Inger Boye

Second Printing, 1959

PRINTED IN THE UNITED STATES OF AMERICA

Contents

v

1

Pelle-Göran Butts the Doctor's Stomach

It was the evening Pelle-Göran punched the doctor in the stomach that it was decided he should go to his grand-mother's, his father's mother.

Now maybe you think that Pelle-Göran must be a real monster, since he would do such a thing as butt the doctor in the stomach. But you are wrong. He was a completely nor-mal and most of the time a rather nice little boy. He was perhaps a little spoiled, being an only child. But when he did this thing, he was terribly upset. He really didn't know what he was doing.

He had been that way ever since a sunny day in April when, for the first time that year, Mamma had brought out the bicycle and taken a spin with him. Mamma had tried to avoid running over a little girl who came dashing across the street. The girl escaped and Pelle-Göran only scratched his knee, but Mamma had landed under a truck. The ambu-lance came and took her off to the hospital.

And from that day on Pelle-Göran had been like a changed boy. He didn't want to eat. He didn't want to play. And he cared nothing for the toys he had liked so well before. He didn't want to obey either. If somebody said he ought to go out, he wanted to stay indoors. But when the weather was bad and they thought he should stay in, he went out. He only wanted to do the opposite of what he was told to do. He thought up some really naughty things, too. He carved on the window sill with his new knife. He cut holes in the curtains. He scribbled the telephone directory full of lines and circles and stiff-legged men. But when Pappa gave him some paper to draw on, he didn't want to draw any more.

Miss Kling who came to clean and cook for Pappa and for him said: "Usch, how much bother boys are! Give me girls any time. They are good."

Perhaps she said it a little too often.

Pelle-Göran had never had anything against girls before. But because she kept on saying it, he became angry with anything that was called a girl. And then he remembered the girl who ran in front of Mamma. It was all *her* fault.

Anyway, he went around angry at everything these days. He was angry at the whole world because his Mamma was ill. Angry at the truck that had run over her. As soon as he spied a truck on the street, he made faces at it, while the driver looked at him very surprised. He hated himself for not having called out: "Watch out, Mamma!" when he saw the truck coming. But he hadn't had time for that.

He was also cross with Miss Kling because she put on Mamma's flowered apron when she washed the dishes. And also because she always insisted on helping him dress in the morning. She said he was too slow. She buttoned his underwear backwards, the way they do it on little children. And he was almost six! He dressed slowly because he didn't feel like getting up any more for everything was so sad.

He was angry because Pappa had to stay at the office all day and leave him alone with Miss Kling. Even so he wasn't much happier when Pappa came home at five o'clock. It was almost as bad because Pappa was sad, too. Once in a while he tried to cheer up Pelle-Göran. He asked if he wanted to play Fortuna or build card houses. But all the time Pelle-Göran felt that Pappa was worrying about Mamma. And that was the thing that was so bad. Something had happened to Mamma's back and legs. It wasn't certain she would ever be able to walk again.

Pelle-Göran wanted his mother so badly, it burned and smarted inside him when he thought about it. He felt so sorry for her. But most of all he felt sorry for himself, because he was *so* lonesome without her.

Several weeks passed before he was allowed to go and visit her in the hospital. After that he could go now and then, sometimes with Pappa, sometimes with Miss Kling. He was always anxious to go, and always sad when some nurse appeared in the door saying that visiting hour was over. The time went altogther too quickly.

He wanted so much to climb up on that big white iron bed with Mamma. But he couldn't do that, he might hurt her. It really was terrible that he could do nothing but pat her cheek and bring her flowers and grapes.

"Dear Mamma, can't you come home?" he begged. "Pappa and I can take care of you. And I'll be so good, so good, if only you'll come home!"

Mamma said that if she were coming home now, perhaps she never would get well. But if she stayed in the hospital, there was a good chance that she would recover.

"Can't I move over here and sleep in that empty bed over there?" he begged.

"Another patient is coming this afternoon and will use that bed," said nurse Asta who was taking care of Mamma.

"Well, can't we take my own bed over here then?" asked Pelle-Göran. "We can ask Mr. Karlson in the fish store to take it here in his truck."

"It is nice that you want to stay with me," said Mamma, "but only sick people may live here."

Pelle-Göran wished he might get sick. He wasn't particularly anxious to get run over—oh, no! But, maybe he could get a little sore throat or something.

One morning he woke up with a sore throat and fever. Oh, how happy he was! But instead of sending him to the hospital Pappa said that nobody who had a cold could go to the hospital. It might be contagious to those who were there. And for a whole week he couldn't go to visit Mamma.

The days were so long. Miss Kling brought oatmeal soup on a tray, fussing at him to eat it all. And then she told some long dull stories about a little girl in a family she had cleaned for. The girl's name was Elsebritt. She had golden hair, and nobody could be nicer than she was, said Miss Kling. Elsebritt never fretted about the food, ate all she was given, and always said: "Oh, my, how good! May I have some more?" And she never sulked either. And very often she would come and give Miss Kling a hug and a kiss on the cheek.

Then Miss Kling asked if Pelle-Göran wouldn't like to go and play with Elsebritt sometime, if Elsebritt's Mamma would let Miss Kling bring Pelle-Göran. But Pelle-Göran glumly said, "Never in my life." He thought that Elsebritt

5

was silly to hug anybody but her Mamma. Anyway, all girls were silly.

"Pelle-Göran, you are a contrary one," said Miss Kling. "Just remember that your Mamma whom you love so much was once a little girl, too."

"Mamma," thought Pelle-Göran. And then he crawled under the cover, head and all, and lay there so homesick for his Mamma he almost cried.

In the afternoon, the first day he was up and around again, Miss Kling was standing in the kitchen, singing and crushing breadcrumbs in time to her singing. Pappa had said Pelle-Göran couldn't go to visit his Mamma before the day after tomorrow. But as he stood there listening to the song, he felt he had to go and see her right away.

Pelle-Göran managed to get hold of his cap in the closet. He didn't care about the jacket. Cautiously he opened the door and hurried down the stairs. He didn't have money for the streetcar, but he knew the route it took. He ran until he was out of breath. Then he walked a little, and then he started running again.

It was beginning to get dark when he reached the hospital. He was lucky. Nobody noticed him as he sneaked in through the door. The great vestibule was empty. He didn't dare take the elevator since he was alone. But he had learned where Mother's room was anyway, for Pappa and he always used the stairs when they walked down. Two nurses were standing chatting in the corridor. Behind their back, and panting heavily, he sneaked into the room with the big number 7 on the door.

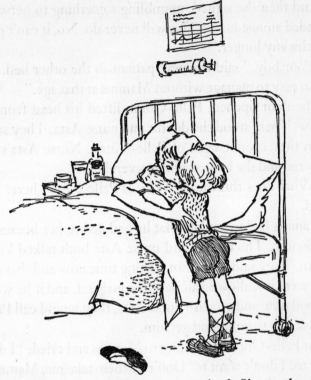

"Pelle-Göran," said Mamma, surprised. She made an attempt to sit up, but fell back again on the pillow. "You here at this hour, and all alone? Does Pappa know?"

But Pelle-Göran tossed his cap on the floor and rushed over to Mamma. He threw his arms around her neck and buried his head in the pillow. He didn't say a word, just held on to her as hard as he could.

Mamma stroked his hair which was damp after all his running.

"My little boy," she whispered.

7

And then she sighed, mumbling something to herself. It sounded almost like: "This will never do. No, it can't go on like this any longer."

"Poor boy," said the new patient in the other bed. "It's not so easy to manage without Mamma at that age."

The door opened. Pelle-Göran lifted his head from the pillow. There stood the doctor and nurse Asta. They stared when they caught sight of Pelle-Göran. Nurse Asta's face grew red and she looked at him severely.

"What does this mean? Why is Pelle-Göran here?" she asked.

Mamma had to explain that he had fled to her because he was lonely. The doctor and nurse Asta both talked kindly to him. They said it was not visiting time now and that children were not allowed alone at the hospital, and if he would be good now and go with nurse Asta, they would call Pappa and ask him to come and get him.

But Pelle-Göran just clung to Mamma and cried: "I don't want to! I don't want to! Don't let them take me, Mamma!"

"But Pelleboy," said Mamma, her voice trembling as if she were very tired. "Run along with nurse Asta now. You can come back some other day."

Nurse Asta tried to pull him away with her. But he struggled against it. Then the doctor wanted to help and tried to lift him up. Then Pelle-Göran became completely wild.

First he butted the doctor in the stomach with his head. Then he kicked nurse Asta on her leg so that she cried out, "Oh!"

And Mamma, crying too, said: "Forgive him. I think he

had a shock that day he saw the car run me down. He hasn't
been himself since then. He never used to behave like this."

"Now, now, quiet, boy," said the doctor, holding on to
him, while nurse Asta ran out and called Pappa.

After a while Pappa came in a taxi to take him home.

"What have you been up to now?" he asked.

Pelle-Göran didn't answer. He only stared unhappily
down at the floor. In low voices Pappa and Mamma talked
with the doctor. Suddenly he heard Pappa say, "I wonder
if it wouldn't be best to send him away for a while. Both his
grandmothers have asked to have him."

"Well, I suppose there isn't any other way," said Mamma,
sounding worried.

"Excellent idea," said the doctor. "That is certainly better than a nursery or a playschool, which I had thought of suggesting."

"I don't *want* to go away," screamed Pelle-Göran.

Then the doctor said, sounding very serious: "Listen to me Pelle, or whatever your name is. You love your Mamma, don't you?"

Pelle-Göran didn't care to answer such a silly question. Of course he loved his Mamma.

"Your Mamma has been very ill," continued the doctor. "She is beginning to get better now. She is almost well enough for us to try—well, a little operation. But if you come up here and upset things in this way, she will be worse again. You understand that, don't you? Look at her! Do you think that acting like this is good for a sick person?"

"I-I-I didn't mean . . ." stuttered Pelle-Göran, looking anxiously at the white face in the bed.

"I know you didn't," said the doctor, a little more gently. "That's why I am telling you how dangerous it is."

"He is so little," said Pappa, "he doesn't have much sense yet."

"Oh, I don't think he is so stupid," said the doctor. "He understands more than you think."

"He feels so lonely without me," said Mamma, trying to excuse him. "You see, doctor, we never had been away from each other before this happened."

The doctor nodded. Then he put his hand on Pelle-Göran's shoulder.

"If you are a good boy and do as I tell you, I will make your Mamma well again," he said. "Will you?"

"Yes, what should I do?" asked Pelle-Göran eagerly.

"Well, I want you to go to your grandmother's and stay there until your Mamma can get home again."

Mamma's mother lived on Aland. Every summer they used to stay with her. He liked his grandmother. He always had such good times there, and he often used to talk about going there on the steamer which was such fun.

But he wanted to stay where Mamma was. And he had gotten into the habit of saying "no" to everything.

"I don't want to go to grandmother on Aland," he cried.

"Is that so," said Pappa grimly. "Well, as you like. Then it will be your other grandmother."

Pelle-Göran looked up. He realized this was serious now. When Pappa used that voice it was no good making any fuss.

"Maybe I should go to grandmother on Aland, anyway," he said meekly. "I have my bark-boats there."

"No, you said no, so no it's going to be," said Pappa. "We have to come to some decision. Now it's settled you are going to your other grandmother."

"And where does this other grandmother live?" asked the doctor.

"In Skane," said Pappa. "On the South Ridge."

"A wonderful place," said the doctor. "You are lucky you can go there. And such good food you get in Skane, too."

For a moment Pelle-Göran forgot that he was sad.

"Grandmother can bake *spettecake*," he said. "She always sends us one for Christmas."

"You don't say," said the doctor. "Spettecake is the best thing I know."

"Me too," said Pelle-Göran.

"Listen, do you suppose we two might arrange something?" said the doctor. "If I make your Mamma quite well, do you think you might persuade your grandmother to bake me a spettecake when you come home again?"

"Are you sure Mamma will get well again?" wondered Pelle-Göran uneasily.

"Quite sure. I and the others here at the hospital will do our best for her. Well, what do you say? Do you think you might get me that spettecake?"

"I'll try," said Pelle-Göran.

"Look me straight in the eyes and shake hands on it!"

They shook hands and looked into each other's eyes.

"Say, Pelleboy, isn't there something else before you go?" came softly from Mamma's bed.

Pelle-Göran understood. He and Mamma always understood one another. He felt very much ashamed.

"Excuse me for butting and kicking you," he said to the doctor and nurse Asta.

"That's all right, son," said nurse Asta.

"Of course I forgive you," said the doctor. "If only you won't do it again."

"Oh, no," Pelle-Göran assured him." You hurt your neck terribly when you butt people like that."

2

The Girl with the Rose

Grandmother came up to Stockholm to get Pelle-Göran, and she stayed on for a few days. She was also going to get another relative, who was on her way down from Norrland, and then the three of them were to go to Skane together.

Pelle-Göran was a little shy with grandmother. It had been so long since he had seen her, he had almost forgotten how she looked. And it was not quite as easy to get acquainted with her again as it had been with his other grandmother.

Grandmother on Aland was round and talkative and quick to laugh. She had curly white hair and a pink face with dimples in her cheeks. And sometimes, when she became especially happy, she would clap her hands and dance around and around, old as she was. And she could think up the most amusing things to do. Yes, grandmother from Aland was his best playmate, next to Mamma, of course.

This grandmother wasn't a bit like her. She was tall, al-

13

most as tall as Pappa. Her dark hair was parted in the middle and combed straight back and tied into a braided knot. She did not talk much to Pelle-Göran. He thought she seemed rather stern as she looked at him with her wise brown eyes. And when he met that glance, as he was sulking or saying "no" to something they wanted him to do, he actually felt himself shrinking. If only he could have gone to his nice cheerful grandmother's. He was sorry he had made that fuss. But it was too late now to regret it.

Grandmother and Pappa were talking about the Norrland relative who was going home with them, and Pelle-Göran understood from what grandmother said that she was a little girl called Katarina. Why couldn't it have been a boy!

"And can you imagine those nice people who own a flowershop were down in Skane this summer, trying to locate some relatives who might take care of her. When they didn't find any, they took her back with them. They didn't think of asking me because I was not a close relative. But as soon as I heard about it I wrote to them. It seems to me they have done enough for the child, especially since it isn't their responsibility."

"Poor little thing, she has been sorely tried," said Pappa. "But are you sure, mother, that you can manage two children at the same time?"

"I used to manage the five of you once upon a time, so—to be sure—I can take care of two little ones like these," said grandmother in her funny Skanish way. "Besides, I think they will take care of each other."

"Do you mean, mother, that Katarina would stay for good?"

"Why not?" said grandmother. "If she likes it there, and we get along well? I have always wanted a little girl, I who had one boy after the other."

Pelle-Göran had listened, but he hadn't understood it all. Why did that girl have to stay with relatives? Why couldn't she live with her Mamma and her Pappa?

And grandmother, he thought, she only likes girls. You could tell that. She is just like Miss Kling. And that Katarina! Of course, she would be just like that Elsebritt, who always is good and nice and hugs and kisses and eats several plates full of pea soup and fat pork. But she'd better not come here and try to hug me. Oh no! Grandmother says we can take care of each other. I am not taking care of *her*. She had better stay up there in Norrland.

"Is it at 8:15 her train will get in?" asked Pappa. "Then I'll just be able to pick her up before going to the office. Would you like to go to the station with me early tomorrow morning and get your little cousin, Pelle-Göran?"

"No," said Pelle-Göran glumly, leaving them.

He certainly didn't intend to drive down and pick up any girl. And when she came, she had better not touch his toys either. There wouldn't be anything but trouble with her, he felt sure. And since grandmother only cared about her, and not a bit about him, he knew it was going to be just as terrible in Skane as here at home.

But the next morning after Pappa had gone to the station, he couldn't help feeling a little curious after all. And while

15

grandmother read the newspaper, he tiptoed out into the hall and hid behind some overcoats hanging there.

"I'll only take a little peek at her," he thought. "Then I'll sneak in and sit behind the writing desk, and I won't come out all day, so that she can see I don't care one bit about her."

He had to wait a long time. Not before he felt his legs getting tired did he hear a car stop at the gate.

And then Pappa stuck the key in the door and came in with her. Cautiously Pelle-Göran peered out between a raincoat and grandmother's black coat.

How surprised he was! He had been expecting a very

small girl, smaller than himself. But this one was almost twice as big as he.

She looked so funny. And how strange her clothes were, winter coat with a fur collar, although it was the beginning of summer. A heavy, coal-black fringe of hair was hanging over her eyes, and she had buried her chin so far down into the fur collar that the fringe of hair and the collar almost met. Not much more than the tip of her nose could be seen. Her coat pockets were packed so full she looked rather wide across the hips. On her long thin legs she wore ribbed woolen stockings, and on her fur collar she had pinned an artificial flower, candy pink and as big as a head of lettuce.

She was standing just inside the door with a small hand-bag in her hand, peeping shyly out from under her fringe of

17

hair. Pappa put down her big bag and called in to grand-mother, "Hello, mother, your little girl is here, and now I have to hurry off to the office."

Grandmother came out and Pappa left.

"Good morning, and welcome, little Katarina," said grandmother holding her arms out to her.

"Well, now the hugging begins," thought Pelle-Göran.

But the girl only lifted her head a little, made a curtsy, and hesitatingly held out a hand to grandmother. A pair of big gray eyes appeared under the fringe of hair peering anxiously at grandmother.

Grandmother took the hand with both of hers and smiled warmly down at her. The girl's eyes looked shy. But when grandmother smiled they began to twinkle a bit. And then finally a really sunny smile broke out between the fur collar and the fringe of hair.

"I was told to bring Mr. and Mrs. Näslund's kind regards and tell you that I can . . ."

Here she stopped, clearing her throat a little. When grandmother didn't say anything, it came a little more tim-idly, "Well, that I could stay as long as you want me."

Grandmother nodded and pushed the fringe out of her eyes.

"But take off your coat, child. You are so warm, you are steaming."

"Oh my, yes, how warm it is here down south," sighed the girl, quickly pulling off her heavy coat.

Grandmother helped her hang it up. She hung it right in front of Pelle-Göran so that he couldn't see anything. As

18

she was doing that, something fell out of one of the stuffed coat pockets and rolled in between his feet.

"What was that?" wondered grandmother.

"Only a bulb," said the girl, quickly bending down to pick it up.

Then she discovered Pelle-Göran's legs.

"Look," she said and began to laugh. "I think there is a little boy hiding behind the clothes."

"Oh, there is?" said grandmother. "Come out, Pelle-Göran. Well, Katarina, this is your cousin, who is going home with us to the South Ridge."

Then, of course he had to come out.

"Hi there," said the girl shaking hands with him.

"He likes playing like that," said grandmother.

"Do I?" thought Pelle-Göran, ashamed at being caught.

"Sometimes I like playing hide and seek, too," said the girl.

Then she began looking for what had fallen out of her coat pocket. Pelle-Göran picked it up and handed it to her. It looked like a kind of an onion. Not the kind used with a steak, but a coarser sort.

"It is a tulip bulb," said the girl. "I have seventeen of them. I almost forgot them when I was going to the train. Mr. Näslund gave them to me. He took them off flowers he sold."

"What are you going to do with bulbs?" Pelle-Göran couldn't keep from asking, although he had decided not to say a word to her.

"I thought I could plant them in front of your place in

Skane, if you'd let me," said the girl looking up anxiously at grandmother.

"Oh my, yes," smiled grandmother. "I'm sure you can do that."

"Not this year, but maybe next year they'll bloom. That's what Mr. Näslund thought," said the girl.

"I'm sure they'll look nice," said grandmother. "But now I think we shall go in and see if we can get us some breakfast and then I think you ought to call me grandmother, Katarina."

"Well, but . . . well," said the girl. And then she stopped.

"Well, if you don't want to say grandmother, you don't have to, of course," said grandmother.

"Oh yes, I only meant that then you and Pelle-Göran could say Kaja, because that's what everybody else says."

"Gladly," said grandmother. "Come on then, Kaja."

Pelle-Göran didn't say anything. Kaja, he thought, sounds just like a bird, a bird that looks like a crow, only smaller. Funny to have a name like that.

But then he got to thinking it would be even funnier to have a name like a church. Because in the south part of Stockholm there was a church called Katarina.

In the door to the dining room Kaja turned around.

"Excuse me, I forgot," she said. "I'll be back right away."

She ran back and soon returned with the pink cloth rose and fastened it on her dress with a safety pin. Grandmother looked puzzled at the rose. She didn't seem to think too much of it.

"Did you get that too from Mr. Näslund?" she asked.

"Oh no," said Kaja. "I got it from a girl called Gertrud. She is my best friend. Her Mamma had it on the nice dress she wore to parties. But then she gave it to Gertrud, and she gave it to me."

"Oh, I understand," said grandmother.

"And I promised that I would wear it all the time I was traveling," said Kaja, "night and day, indoors and out."

"Well, what one has promised, one must keep, of course," said grandmother.

"And I gave Gertrud a real rose which Mr. Näslund had given me, because I ran two errands with some wreaths for him. And when it withers Gertrud is going to press it and keep it as long as she lives."

"Oh," said grandmother, "that sounds nice. And now let us eat. You want a dish of oatmeal, don't you, Kaja?"

"Thank you, but just a small one," said Kaja.

Then she was not such a big eater as Elsebritt, thought Pelle-Göran, who was so busy looking at this new cousin, that he didn't notice that he put away a big load of oatmeal.

"How old are you?" he asked.

"Eleven years next month. And I know you are five, because that was what grandmother wrote."

"Six, soon," said Pelle-Göran quickly.

He didn't go in and hide behind the desk as he had thought of doing. Miss Kling was packing his bags. And now he began bringing out all kinds of things he didn't think he could do without.

"You can't drag along your whole toybox to Skane," said Miss Kling. "There isn't room, you understand."

21

But grandmother came to his aid.

"Children ought to be allowed to take along a few toys," she said firmly. "Let him put in what he likes best."

So Miss Kling let him put in the fire truck, the little blue car and the book, *The Tomtebo Children*. But when he brought the black dachshund and the baby lion, she slammed the lid and locked the case, saying it was full. Then he grew so angry he thought he would go and sit behind the desk after all. But Kaja came and whispered to him that the baby lion and the dachshund might stay in her big suitcase, for there would surely be room, if only he would help her afterwards and sit on the lid so she could get it locked. And that's what he did. They had to open it once because a pajama leg was hanging out. The second time only part of a belt was visible, and Kaja said that didn't matter.

3

Rhyming in a Sleeping Car

Late in the evening they started off. Pappa took them to the train.

"Mamma and I and the doctor expect you to be very nice to grandmother and Kaja," he whispered to Pelle-Göran when they said good-bye.

"I'll try," mumbled Pelle-Göran.

And then the train started. Sleeping car. They were traveling in a sleeping car! Pelle-Göran had never done that before. But Kaja took it calmly. She had traveled all alone in a sleeping car all the way from Umea.

When Pelle-Göran entered the sleeping compartment he saw only two beds, one above the other.

"Where am I going to sleep?" he said.

"Up there, I had thought," said grandmother. "I would rather not climb ladders."

"But what about her," he said, pointing to Kaja.

"Kaja and you will have to bunk together in the upper

bed," said grandmother. "Two children can share one bed when traveling on a train."

"Noho," said Pelle-Göran indignantly. "She isn't going to stay in my bed."

"No, but perhaps you can stay in hers, if you are good," said grandmother, laughing a little.

"I want to go home," said Pelle-Göran angrily.

"You do? That might not be so easy," said grandmother.

He peered through the window. The train was just passing over a bridge. He saw only water down below. And the train was going fast.

Grandmother opened her bag and began taking out what she needed for the night.

"I can tell you, though, that there is plenty of space up there," she said quietly. "The bunk is long and each of you can have his own part of it and try not to kick."

Pelle-Göran climbed up the ladder and looked at the bed. Well, it certainly wasn't short. But to lie in the same bed as Kaja! He had always had a bed to himself.

Kaja was hanging up her coat.

"It will be all right, you'll see," she said when he came down again. "I promise to be as quiet as a mouse in a house, as a rat in a flat, as a . . ."

"Can you rhyme?" he asked surprised.

"Yes, can you?"

"Of course. My Mamma and I rhyme all the time. Mamma reads the book *Hattstugan* to me. That's where I learned to rhyme."

"Make a rhyme then, so I can hear if you can do it," said

24

Kaja. "Say, how quiet you can lie in bed."

Pelle-Göran thought a little.

"As a witch in a ditch," he said, letting himself down on the lower bed.

"Fine," said Kaja and sat down beside him. "Shall we have a rhyming race? As a pig in a wig, I say."

"As a dog in a fog," said Pelle-Göran.

"As a cat in a hat," said Kaja.

"As a burro in a furrow," said Pelle-Göran.

"As a skunk in a trunk," said Kaja.

"Usch, that was terrible," said Pelle-Göran. "I say, as a bird in a word."

"Then I'll say as a fish in a dish," said Kaja.

Grandmother turned around.

"As a hen in a pen," she rhymed.

Pelle-Göran stared at her.

"Can *you* make up rhymes, grandmother?" he said astonished.

"Oh yes," said grandmother. "I'm not so stupid I can't do that."

"It's your turn now, Pelle-Göran," said Kaja.

"As a gnat on a bat," he said.

"As a bear at a fair," said Kaja, "and now it is grandmother's turn."

"As a fox in a box," said grandmother and began taking out Pelle-Göran's night clothes.

"As a cod on a rod," said Pelle-Göran.

"As a flea in the tea," said Kaja.

Pelle-Göran began to laugh so uproariously at the flea in

the tea that grandmother said: "As sleep in a heap. And now it will have to be enough with rhyming for tonight. In bed with you children! We must change trains very early tomorrow morning since we couldn't get tickets to the car going straight through."

"As an adder on a ladder," sang Kaja as she climbed up into the berth and moved the pink rose from her coat to her pajama top.

"Listen," said Pelle-Göran, when he had brushed his teeth and stretched out on the bed. "I'll tell you I made a real poem once." But the train was making so much noise that Kaja could not hear what he said. So he crawled over to her and said the verse into her ear:

> "Did you see a chicken eat
> A herring like a piece of meat?"

Kaja said that was quite a good poem, but they'd better go to sleep now. And then she pulled down the little silver shutter over the lamp she had above her pillow. It became dark, and Pelle-Göran crawled back again.

Grandmother had already turned off her lamp. Only outside from the corridor came a faint yellow light.

But he couldn't sleep. The train clattered and clanged over the tracks, the walls around him creaked and crackled, and the bed was unusually hard. He turned and twisted and thought about Mamma at the hospital and that now he was going farther and farther away from her.

Suppose she didn't get well at all? If that operation didn't help? Suppose she would have to stay at the hospital the

rest of her life? Then he would have to stay with grandmother and never go home again. For he was supposed to
stay until Mamma became well again. Suppose she never got
well?

Thinking about all this he began feeling so bad that he
would just as soon have jumped off the train and run on
home. But since he knew he couldn't do that he began to
cry softly. What was he doing on this noisy, silly train anyway? A sleeping car wasn't at all as nice as he had thought
it might be. Sometimes the train stopped with a jerk and he
almost rolled halfway around. Kaja was lying as still as a
mouse, as she had said, but her legs got in the way when he
tried to stretch out diagonally across the bed, as he usually
did. When he was crying the hardest, the lamp over Kaja

was lighted. He saw her sit up, looking at him. Then she began digging into the little bag she had put on the shelf above the bed. Finally she got out two shiny red apples, and one of them she rolled over to him. Then she waved good night and pushed down the little shutter.

So they lay there, munching and eating, while the train rolled south and the early summer night turned grey outside. They were good apples. They tasted like honey. And when Pelle-Göran had sucked the last drop of juice from the core of the apple, he let it fall down on the floor, since he didn't know what to do with it. Then he fell asleep and slept soundly the whole night, until in the morning the conductor rapped on the door, calling out, "We'll be in Hässleholm in thirty-five minutes."

They hurriedly got up. Grandmother was already up. She had washed and was just putting on her shoes.

Through the compartment window the morning sun was sending clusters of long golden needles, making shimmering rainbows on the big decanter filled with water. Pelle-Göran washed and dressed himself. He buttoned his underwear in the front and thought how nice it was that Miss Kling was not there. He did expect grandmother to grow impatient and begin helping him, as he was so slow. But she didn't. And he did get finished in time.

They packed their night things and Kaja moved her cloth rose over on her fur collar again. And then they were in Hässleholm, standing in the crowded corridor with the other passengers trying to get out.

They had some time to wait before the next train left. So

28

grandmother took them to the station coffee shop where they had cocoa and fresh sweet rolls.

"Do you want whipped cream with it?" asked the lady who served them.

"I should say so," said grandmother emphatically.

She herself drank coffee and read a Skanish newspaper which was lying on the table. And then it was time to continue the journey.

On the new train you could feel at once in which part of the country you were. It was filled with wide-awake people, all speaking Skanish. And the conductor greeted grandmother like an old acquaintance, saying: "It sure must be grand up there on the South Ridge now, Mrs. Bengtsson?"

"It isn't too bad up yonder at Stockholm either," said grandmother, smiling warmly.

Just imagine, all of a sudden she spoke much more Skanish than she had done before. And in Stockholm Pappa also had started speaking more Skanish as soon as grandmother had arrived.

Pelle-Göran looked respectfully at grandmother thinking she certainly must be an important person since she knew the conductor. And as she sat there at the window, watching the landscape they were traveling through, she looked so kind and nice he did not feel like a stranger towards her any more. He went over and stood beside her with his hand on her shoulder and watched with her. Kaja stuck her morning tousled head in beside him and watched also.

"Have you been here before, Pelle-Göran?" she asked.

"Yes, but I was so small, I don't remember it. Have you?"

"Last summer we just about drove all over Skane," she said.

"Not alone, though?" wondered Pelle-Göran. "Your Pappa and your Mamma were with you, weren't they?"

Kaja's face turned red.

"It was Mr. and Mrs. Näslund who were along," she said.

She turned abruptly and walked over to the other side of the car, where she stood with her back to them looking out. Pelle-Göran stared questioningly at her dark head. He couldn't understand why she acted so strange.

Grandmother took his hand and pulled him close to her.

"Kaja's Pappa and Mamma died when she was little," she said in his ear. "Then she went to her aunt, but last year her aunt also died. So now Kaja is all alone in the world. And I had thought that you and I and Folke might help her a little."

Pelle-Göran didn't know what to answer. But he pressed grandmother's hand a little before he let go.

Such a terrible thing! No Pappa and no Mamma. And still she could laugh and be happy sometimes!

But right now she didn't look happy at all. She had buried her face in the warm fur collar just the way she had done that time she came in through the door at home. He was feeling so sorry for her, but he didn't know what he could do to make her happy again.

He looked at grandmother. She nodded encouragingly. So he went over to Kaja and touched her arm. "Do you like cars?" he said. "Would you like to have my little blue one? You can have it if you want it. But maybe you'd let me play with it sometimes?"

"Sure," she said. "Thank you."

But she said it so quietly, she almost mumbled it. So she couldn't be really happy, not yet. Perhaps she didn't think much of the little blue car.

"Or maybe you would rather have the fire truck?" he asked, his head drooping a little. For the fire truck was terribly nice and almost brand new.

Then she smiled a little and said: "Thank you, but you know, I think that little blue one is the very nicest one."

"Then you may have that," he said relieved.

The train stopped at a station and a little old woman carrying a basket came into the car. She sat down beside another woman sitting at one of the windows. The two of them were old friends and immediately began to talk together. One of them was a little deaf, and they spoke so loudly, the whole car could hear what they were saying. The woman with the basket said, "I'm on my way to Fritzine Assarsson with kittens."

"Kittens!" said the other one. "Let's see."

The woman with the basket lifted the lid just a little. Two tiny kittens peeked out. They mewed and scratched trying to get out of their prison.

The next moment Kaja was there. She knelt down on the dusty floor looking in delight at the small struggling mites. She certainly didn't look sad any longer.

"Pelle-Göran, come and look," she cried.

He hurried over and helped her admire the sweet little things.

"Do you like pussy cats?" he asked.

"I think more than anything else," answered Kaja.

"Don't you have a cat?" asked the owner.

"No," said Kaja. "But when I grow up, I'm going to have one, that's for sure."

"Well, it's no trouble getting them. It's a little harder getting rid of the crop, I can tell you, little lady."

The two women laughed and then they began talking about somebody called Dagny who had a new deep-freeze, and that was something everybody certainly ought to have, they felt, if they had the money for it. Kaja and Pelle-Göran played with the kittens until the woman put the lid on the basket and got off the train.

Kaja walked over to grandmother and asked her if she had any animals. "Yes, I have some, of course," said grandmother. "Not so many, though. But you will see, when we get there."

"Oh, I am so glad," said Kaja.

"I like animals, too, if only they are good," said Pelle-Göran. "Not the kind that bites."

"I have only nice animals," said grandmother. "And if you look out the window now, you'll see the South Ridge."

On the left side of the railroad rose a long forest-clad hill.

"Such beautiful trees. Are they beeches?" wondered Kaja.

"There are all kinds of trees, beech and spruce and oak. Most of them are beeches but little by little, I'm afraid, the spruce is winning over the beech."

"That green over there looks like a nice bunch of parsley," said Pelle-Göran, pointing to some trees.

Grandmother laughed.

"When I was a child, I too thought that the oak groves looked like parsley from a distance."

But Kaja said in a low voice, "My aunt liked parsley so much. She chopped it and used it on sandwiches. She said that if people would eat parsley and cloudberries and things like that every day, they would stay healthy. We always did it, but auntie became ill and died anyway."

"She was a teacher, wasn't she?" asked grandmother, patting Kaja's hand.

33

"Yes, and she was so good," said Kaja, hiding her face in the fur collar again. "I guess all nice people die," she mumbled.

"Sooner or later we shall all die, whether we are good or bad," said grandmother. "But it is only when we are good that we shall be missed afterwards."

Pelle-Göran did not at all like the way they were talking. He was beginning to get hot and impatient.

"Aren't we nearly there?" he asked again and again, moving restlessly around.

"Soon," said grandmother.

But it was still a little way to go. During the time Kaja taught him to play "Hammer and nail." They clapped and they clashed the palms of their hands against the hands of the other, and sometimes they missed. But they kept on until grandmother got up and began taking down the bags. "We aren't far off now," she said.

4

Folke, Lubbe, and the Wise
Goose Amelie

The train rolled into the station and stopped. Grandmother leaned out of the window and waved to somebody
out there.

"Here you have us, Folke," she called.

And grandmother's youngest son, who was so young that
Pelle-Göran didn't have to call him uncle, came on board
the train to help his mother down with the children and the
luggage.

Folke didn't look like grandmother or Pappa at all. He
was short with broad shoulders and just a little chubby. His
thick, curly hair shone like yellow straw, and his eyes were
just as blue as his shirt. He was so sunburnt Pelle-Göran
thought he'd never seen anything like it.

"Welcome to the South Ridge," said Folke. "It's going
to be nice to have young ones on the old Stubba Farm. I
have been the baby far too long."

Kaja, who had cautiously stayed behind grandmother,

ventured forth when he held out his hand to her. She blushed with pleasure when he said, "How nice of you to come all this way to see us. Now we'll have to make sure you have a good time, and won't be sorry you came."

"I'm so glad," she stammered.

"And you, Pelle-Göran, you have grown. I suppose you have forgotten me, haven't you?"

"Noho," said Pelle-Göran.

He really had forgotten Folke, but now, when he saw him, he suddenly remembered that once a very long time ago, he had ridden on those broad shoulders and held on to that yellow shock of hair.

"When I was little I used to call you Tolte," he said.

"That's right," said Folke. "I remember that, too."

He spoke slowly and calmly, and he walked firmly with wide steps as he carried all the bags over to the car. One could see he knew what he wanted and meant what he said. It wasn't hard to understand that he was cheerful either, for he had laughing wrinkles around his eyes.

When he asked grandmother how the trip had been, she answered, "Oh, it went fine, but just the same, it will be good to get home again."

The car wasn't so terribly fine or up-to-date but it was a car, nevertheless. Pelle-Göran liked all cars except trucks. His Pappa didn't have one yet. Perhaps next summer, he had said when Pelle-Göran had begged.

"Well, I suppose you want to sit up here with me," said Folke, just as if he were reading Pelle-Göran's thoughts.

And then he heaved Pelle-Göran into the front seat. Grandmother and Kaja had to climb in the back.

"Now we are driving up on the Ridge," said Folke when they had left the station behind and driven for awhile.

Gently curving, the road slowly rose through light green beech woods with sunlight sprinkled in among new leaves and silky, shiny trunks. Last year's leaves covered the ground in drifts, changing from brick red, rusty brown to rose red. It was so beautiful that Pelle-Göran even forgot to look at the wheel and the trembling speedometer which he always watched when he was allowed to sit up front.

"Look, what a funny little dog," he said, when a grayish brown animal with long hind legs jumped across the road.

"That was a rabbit," said Folke.

"Oh, can't we stop and look at it?" cried Kaja.

But the rabbit was already far away, in among the trees.

"You will see many rabbits," said grandmother. "We have lots of them around Stubba Farm."

They drove on again, the road still climbing upwards.

"Are we going higher?" wondered Pelle-Göran.

"Sure," said Folke. "Those who say Skane is flat have not been on the South Ridge."

"I am sure Kaja, coming from the North, has seen higher places," said grandmother.

But Kaja never had time to answer that, for now they were there. To the right, the forest opened up. One could see many miles across meadows, fields and glens covered with heavy foliage. In the distance sparkled the Sound, and still farther away, on the blue horizon, was "The Danish Land," as grandmother said in answer to Kaja's surprised question.

"The finest thing we have here is the view," she said.

"And next to it comes the glen," said Folke.

"The glen? What's that?"

"The glen? Well, you people from up north just call it a dell," said Folke. "It's a narrow woody valley with a stream. You'll soon see."

A stone fence, half-covered with climbing blackberry tendrils, separated the land belonging to Stubba Farm from the highway. Farther in one caught a glimpse of some long red houses, built around a square yard. Straw thatched roofs covered with green moss came down over the low sides. And like a dome, the old oak trees lifted their rippling leafy crowns far above the buildings.

Folke stepped out of the car and opened the gate. Suddenly something big and black and shaggy rushed past him and jumped up on the car with wild howls of joy. And close behind came something white, fluttering and quacking. There was a flurry of black fur and white wings, of a red open mouth and a clattering yellow beak. And the noise they were making even drowned out the dull rumbling of the old engine.

Grandmother had to open the door and receive the wildly enthusiastic greetings. Then, while Pelle-Göran knelt on the front seat, to see what kind of creatures they were and Kaja screamed with delight, they were introduced to the Newfoundland dog, Lubbe, and the old wise goose,

Amelie, who was twelve years old, and had stopped laying eggs a long time ago, but was never going to be butchered, because she was just like a family friend.

"These are our grandchildren," said grandmother to the animals. "Say hello now, and tell them they are welcome to Stubba Farm."

But instead of greeting them, Lubbe jumped right into the car and Amelie followed him at once, as if she had done nothing all her life but travel in cars. They sniffed and touched the children a little, but not much. Then dog and goose both put their heads in grandmother's lap, looking up at her with such adoring eyes that everyone could understand she had really been missed. And so Folke drove into the yard with his menagerie.

Kaja's face was shining, and she stealthily patted Lubbe's black fur. Lubbe didn't pay any attention, but Amelie stretched her neck and hissed warningly at the girl.

"Shame on you, Amelie," said grandmother, tapping the goose on the beak.

She calmed down then, but she still glared a bit at Kaja with her bright eyes which slanted a little above her round cheeks.

"Lubbe and Amelie are best friends, and Amelie is always afraid that someone might hurt Lubbe. She is defending him," said grandmother.

It sounded very funny to have a goose defending a dog as big as a bear. But now the car had reached the entrance, and both people and animals got out. Later on there was so much else to see and to think about that they almost forgot the dog and the goose.

A smiling and kind looking little old woman stood on the front stairs, "Welcome home, dear Klara," she said. "Welcome, dear children!"

"This is my old friend and cousin, Dela," said grandmother. "Adela is her name, but we call her Dela. She is a widow, just as I am, and she lives here with me."

The dog and the goose stayed nicely outside while grandmother took the children to their room and Folke carried up their bags. They had a gabled room in the attic. The wallpaper was faded and there was no regular ceiling. The straw thatched roof with the big center beam was fully visible. In the small window stood a red geranium, and the floor was covered with gay striped rag rugs. At each long wall was a bed. Also in the room were a table, a few chairs, a chest of drawers, a washstand with a blue flowered washbowl and a pitcher, and two old chests, one red, one blue.

"This one your grandfather made when your father was born," said grandmother to Pelle-Göran pointing to the blue chest. "Now you may put your toys and all your secrets in it. The red one comes from my childhood home. That's going to be Kaja's now."

On the table stood a little vase. Kaja put her rose there, just as if it had been a living flower.

"And now I think you had better change into something cooler, for it's going to be warm today," said grandmother, helping Kaja to look for a cotton dress in her big bag. The dress was too short for her and Kaja's legs looked even longer and thinner when she got it on.

"We'll put away your winter clothes in mothballs," said grandmother, taking charge of the heavy coat and the wool dress.

Pelle-Göran was leaning out of the window. He saw a strip of silvery water shining deep down in the heavily wooded area south of the farm.

"Is there a lake down there?" he asked.

"No, that's our brook," said grandmother. "It is called the Halla brook and it runs out into Vege river."

"Rönne river, Vege river, Kävlinge river," mumbled Kaja, who had read about the Skanish rivers in geography. "Can we go swimming in the brook?"

Folke who just put down the last bag said: "Yes, I'll take you down the glen and show you where the bottom is good."

"Pappa said that the nightingale used to sing in the glen and that's where you pick hazel nuts. Let's go there," said Pelle-Göran pulling at Folke's trouser legs.

"We'll have to eat first," said Folke. "I think Dela has prepared some food for us. After that I'll have to go out with the tractor for a while."

"There'll be time enough for the glen," said grandmother. "The nightingale doesn't sing before tonight, and the nuts won't be ripe before fall. Just wash your hands now before we go down."

When they passed through the entrance hall they saw Lubbe and Amelie waiting faithfully outside the open door.

"What can I do to make friends with Amelie?" asked Kaja.

"You children may take the food to her and to Lubbe, and you'll soon be friends," said grandmother. "But you'd better not play around too roughly with Lubbe for awhile, because if you do, Amelie might come along and give you a pinch."

They ate in the kitchen. There was a huge range, placed inside something that looked like a whitewashed grotto made of big, uneven stones. Grandmother also had an electric plate, but she only used that for her morning coffee. In the kitchen there was a trap door leading down to the cellar.

On a large drop-leaf table stood a wonderful breakfast,

dark, coarse bread with butter, ham and scrambled eggs with small sausages and mashed potatoes. It all tasted delicious. The milk was yellow and rich like cream and wonderfully cool, since it had just been taken up from the cellar. The children needed no urging. They ate as if they were starved and grandmother and Dela both looked pleased.

But the one who finally emptied all the dishes was Folke. Pelle-Göran had never seen anybody who could put away as much food as he. The heaped plate was empty in a hurry and filled time and again. Seeing Pelle-Göran's surprise, Folke laughed.

"Food is good," he said, "and why leave something for the pigs when you can be the pig in the house yourself. The pigs get what they need anyway."

When they had eaten, Folke disappeared. Grandmother took the children over the house. The rooms were low ceil-

43

inged and most of them were quite small. All the windows were filled with flowers and glasses with slips and cuttings which would grow into new plants. In every room there was a rocking chair and an overstuffed davenport. On three of the walls in Folke's room hung framed maps of Skane. On the fourth hung several small and big guns. A row of glass jars containing different samples of grain stood on the desk. The bookcase was filled with books on animal care.

Kaja stared at the guns.

"Are those guns for hunting?" she asked timidly.

"Yes, that's what they are," said grandmother. "The big one is an elk rifle and the others are used for birds and other animals. Most of the men here at the South Ridge go hunting. We have plenty of wildlife here, and if nobody went after them, the foxes and rabbits would become too numerous."

Kaja looked unhappy, but she didn't say anything more about it.

In Dela's room they found a loom with a half-finished Skanish rug. Grandmother explained that Dela earned her living weaving rugs and carpets for the Craft Center. She was clever at sewing, too, and she had promised to make dresses for both grandmother and Kaja.

Striped covers were on all the furniture in the big room and the chandelier hanging from the ceiling was wrapped in tulle. On the walls hung large photographs of grandfather and his parents, and of grandmother's parents as bride and groom. Then there was a huge piano, so big it almost reached the ceiling. There was also a walnut chiffo-

nier, and on the pulled-out leaf stood a great many porcelain figures, angels, shepherds, shepherdesses, two small dogs and a cat, and a little boy pushing a wheelbarrow filled with pink flowers. The biggest figure was a fine porcelain hen sitting on eggs in a basket. Yes, there were lots of things to look at.

But the best of all they found in grandmother's room, where the walls, the table and the chest of drawers were covered with photographs of her children and grandchildren. Swinging back and forth on a ring was a green parrot, and he was just as happy to see grandmother as Lubbe and Amelie had been.

"Hahaha!" he called out and flew over to grandmother's shoulder and began ruffling up her hair. "Hi there, little

Julius! Do you want a bite of food, little Julius? Good night to you, sleep well, little Julius!"

Then he cocked his head and peered thoughtfully at the children.

"Hi there, little Julius," he said again.

"Julius is his own name," said grandmother, patting the parrot on his head.

Suddenly Julius pulled a hairpin out of grandmother's knot, and fluttered over to the gilded cage at the window and climbed through the small open door.

"You mustn't do that," laughed grandmother, sticking her hand in, and trying to get the pin back again. There was a playful tug of war between them. But grandmother won and stuck the pin back in her hair again. The parrot turned his back on her with a peevish, "Hahaha."

They could not get Julius to talk after that. He didn't care even when grandmother said, "Little Julius, we are friends, aren't we?" He didn't even look at her. The children called and coaxed: "Julius! Julius!" But he just pretended he didn't hear.

Then grandmother bent her head close to the cage and for a moment her knot of hair came within the reach of Julius. Quick as a flash he was there and grabbed one of her hairpins again.

"Well, I suppose you'll have to keep that one," said grandmother.

Julius placed the pin across the pole he used to sit on, and put his foot on it. He looked around proudly as if he had accomplished a great deed.

"He takes all my hairpins and hides them behind his water bowl," said grandmother. "Sometimes when he is up before I am, he picks up all of them from the night table. Then he arranges them and plays with them like a boy with his building blocks."

"Can he say anything else?" wondered Kaja.

"No, he can't. Maybe you can teach him. Folke and I haven't much time to stop and talk to him."

"I'll think of something very good," said Kaja.

Pelle-Göran said he would think of something good, too. But now he thought they ought to go outside.

"Oh yes, down to the barn," said Kaja.

"The cows are out right now," said grandmother. "But I think you'll find a couple of little calves there. And there are cats there, too. And kittens. Each of you may choose a kitten, if you like."

"That can't be true," said Kaja, turning quite pale. "Are we . . . am I going to have my own kitten?"

"Sure you are," said grandmother. "But you can't have it in the house. They must stay in the barn, because they have to learn to catch rats there. That's why we keep them."

"Come on, Kaja," said Pelle-Göran impatiently.

And Kaja came. No, she flew.

"Sleep well, little Julius!" called the parrot after them.

"The barn is right there to the left," grandmother said. "And remember not to take the newborn ones. Take the ones that are six weeks old. The small ones must stay with their mother a while yet."

5

Tigerpaw, Rosenose and
Ola Gädda

When the children arrived at the barn they found three
little calves in a stall. "Moo, moo-oo-oo!" They stopped for
a moment to look at them. The calves were mooing and rubbing against the gate into the stall, and it looked as if they
were begging for something. But Kaja hurried on, because
she had caught a glimpse of something even nicer.

In one of the empty stalls lay a striped cat feeding four
newly born kittens. Farther down in a stream of sunlight
some bigger kittens were playing, while a black and white
Mamma cat sat watching them. Kaja stopped, her hands
clasped together. It was a big moment in her life, choosing
her first pet.

"Hurry up and come, Pelle-Göran! Which one do you
want?"

"The black one—no, that little grey one—no, I really
don't know . . ."

"They are nice, all of them," said Kaja bewildered.

48

"Not that one," said Pelle-Göran. "That one is ugly."

It really wasn't very pretty. It had reddish yellowish fur, and one ear was black. The other ear was hanging down, not standing up straight, as a cat's ear ought to do.

"Look at the black one with the white bib," said Kaja. "I almost think . . ."

"Yes, that one is the nicest one," said Pelle-Göran.

"You take that one then," said Kaja. "I'll take a grey one."

Pelle-Göran hesitated.

"Poor little red one whom nobody wants," he said. "It's too bad you are so ugly."

"Kissemissemiss!" called Kaja, trying to attract one of the grey ones.

"But he looks funny anyway, even if he is ugly," said Pelle-Göran. "I could play that he was a tiger."

The red one came running towards him. It cocked its head as if it wondered about him and pricked up its black ear.

"Look, what a nice ear he has. It's just like velvet," said Pelle-Göran. "And look, I think he likes me!"

For the kitten rubbed softly against his bare legs as if it wanted to pet him.

"Meow?" it mewed in a questioning tone. "Meow?"

That decided it.

"I'm taking this one," he said, carefully lifting it up. "Little pussy cat, you are going to be my own little cat, and your name will be Tigerpaw."

"And this one is mine," said Kaja lifting one of the gray ones down from the feeding table. "See how nice it is, light

49

gray, just like silver, and a pink nose. I know what its name is going to be, Rosenose!"

Tigerpaw was struggling and showing its claws.

"He is as wild as a real tiger," said Pelle-Göran trying to unhook its small sharp claws from his jacket.

But when Kaja showed him how he was supposed to hold a cat, it became calmer.

They carried Tigerpaw and Rosenose in to grandmother to show her which ones they had chosen. She looked in surprise at Tigerpaw, but said they had chosen well and that the names weren't bad either. Tigerpaw would certainly become an excellent mouser. One could see that from his color. And then they got some cream in a dish to give to the kittens out in the yard. The Mamma cat came out and walked around them to see that the young ones

were all right. She said something to them in the cat language and then went back to the barn.

Afterwards the children played with the kittens. They tied a cork to a string and let them run after it on the grass. Kaja could think of nothing but Rosenose. She played with it until it fell asleep in her lap and then she could not bear to move. But Tigerpaw sneaked back into the barn so then Pelle-Göran went exploring.

At one end of the barn stood Lubbe's house. Lubbe was not chained, as all the other watch dogs were on the South Ridge. Grandmother said it was cruel to keep animals chained. And Folke said that those who had their watch dogs tied up in a doghouse the year around ought to try it themselves on a cold winter night. Lubbe ran loose day and night, because, said grandmother, he was a steady old dog who didn't bother anybody except the fox if it might come to call on them to get a chicken or two. In winter he stayed in the stable. The doghouse was his summer residence, which he shared with Amelie. As Pelle-Göran went past, the old goose just happened to come out of the house to make sure he didn't touch Lubbe, who was resting on the grass.

Pelle-Göran went around the corner, for he heard the sound of an axe behind the building. He thought it was Folke. But it was only an old man standing there, chopping wood so it sang. He was in his shirt sleeves, but had on a heavy padded vest and on his head he wore a cap with a visor. His eyebrows were as bushy as a mustache, and he looked cross.

"Oh, so here comes the Stockholmer," he said, when Pelle-Göran greeted him.

"What are you doing?" asked Pelle-Göran.

"Chopping wood, as anybody can see," said the old man crossly.

"For grandmother?"

"Who else?" said the old man.

"Do you live here on Stubba Farm, too?"

"Cottage over there," said the old man, pointing with his elbow. Pelle-Göran saw a glimpse of a little house behind some fruit trees on the other side of the stone fence.

"How does he fare, ye're pop up in Stockholm?" asked the old man.

"Fine," said Pelle-Göran. "It's Mamma who is ill."

"Yes, womenfolks have their troubles," said the old man.

"My name is Pelle-Göran. What's yours?"

"Don't matter," said the old codger, placing another piece of wood on the block.

Pelle-Göran looked puzzled. This was something he didn't quite understand.

"Are you mad at me?" he asked.

The old man had lifted up the axe, but now he let it fall and looked at the boy.

"Laddie, the questions ye can ask," he said. "Am I mad at ye? No, I can't say that I am. But I'm old, that I am. And ye'd better stay out o' my way. I'm tired of boys. I don't hold with boys, and now ye hear it. And Ola Gädda is the name if ye have to know it."

Then he let the axe fall, cutting the piece of wood in two so that bits of it flew several yards off.

"My, you sure know how to do that," said Pelle-Göran admiringly. "When I get big, I'm going to buy myself a shiny chopper like that and chop firewood with it."

"What would ye do with an axe? No, ye won't be a wood chopper, no. Ye'll be a fine gentleman like ye're pop, and sit in an office," said Ola Gädda gloomily.

"I am going to be a fire chief," said Pelle-Göran. "I want to drive a red fire engine and throw water on fires. But I can chop wood in between, when there isn't a fire."

"Yes, yes, just go away now, so ye don't get hit in the head by one of these pieces of wood," said Ola Gädda. "Ye go and bother Folke Bengtsson a spell now."

"But I don't know where Folke is," said Pelle-Göran.

53

"He is over there driving the tractor," said the old man, pointing with his elbow.

"Oh yes, good-bye then," said Pelle-Göran holding out his hand.

Ola Gädda raised his mustache-like eyebrows several inches. He looked at the small hand and the polite smile. Then he dried his own big fist on his pants and took the boy's hand as carefully as if it were made of glass.

"Good-bye," he mumbled.

Pelle-Göran hurried off. The old man stood looking after him a while before he bent down for another piece of wood.

6

The Cuckoo Sings

Pelle-Göran didn't have far to go before he met Folke coming down the road. His shirt was open and the perspiration was running down his face.

"I think I promised to take you down the glen," he said. "That will be just fine, for I need to cool off a bit."

They went over and got Kaja who had a hard time tearing herself away from her kitten. But when she heard they were going swimming, she carried Rosenose over to her mother and sisters and brothers in the barn, and hurried for her bathing suit. Meanwhile Folke went down in the cellar and brought up a bottle of blackberry juice, and grandmother split some fresh rolls and spread honey in between. She arranged them in a basket and handed it to Pelle-Göran.

"A bite of food for two hungry men and a skinny little girl," she said.

Two hungry men! Pelle-Göran straightened up. If that didn't sound like something. And my, it smelled good from that basket.

Folke and the children followed a winding, twisting path down the steep slope where young beeches and hazel bushes grew so thickly that at times they walked in a mystical green twilight, and were forced to push aside the branches in order to go on. In the open clearings where the sun reached in, buttercups together with vetch and forget-me-nots, were shining in the mossy grass. A soft, rippling sound was heard from the brook. The very sound was cooling.

"Sh-sh!" said Kaja and stopped. "What's that?"

"Hoho! Hoho!"

"A cuckoo," said Folke. "A cuckoo from the east means ours troubles have ceased! That means an end to our troubles, if we have any. I think we ought to ask him something about our future."

When the cuckoo became silent, Folke began singing the old question song:

"Cuckoobird,
Have you heard,
How long I tarry
Before I marry?"

They listened tensely. For a few minutes there was silence. Then the cuckoo started calling again. Seven times it called.

"Seven years," said Folke. "So, it is going to take that long before I get myself a wife. Well, the one who waits for something good, never waits too long. Now, it's your turn to ask, Kaja."

Kaja hesitated, but then she screwed up her courage and

56

sang the question song. When the cuckoo heard her he began calling back. It was seven calls this time, too.

"It's going to be seven years for you, too. Then maybe you are the one who will be my wife," said Folke, jokingly.

"No thank you," said Kaja, frowning. "I don't want a husband who kills animals. I have seen those guns of yours."

"Aha!" said Folke. "So that's why you have been angry with me. I noticed something was wrong."

Kaja didn't answer.

"Aren't *you* going to ask the cuckoo?" she asked Pelle-Göran.

He didn't want to, but the cuckoo called anyway. It called and called its gentle hoho while they were climbing down to the water.

"Well, here you have the Halla brook," said Folke.

Willows trailed their branches in the green glittering water, and the sandy bottom was white and smooth in the little bay he pointed out as the best place to swim. The brook was quite wide just there. On the bottom big stones were strewn all around.

"You are safe here, but its muddy on the sides, and a little farther out there are deep holes and pits where you can't feel the bottom," Folke said. "Always remember to stay inside those stones. Promise me that."

They promised. Kaja could swim, but she promised it

anyway. It is easy to promise. To keep a promise is some-times more difficult.

But this time they kept what they had promised. Quickly they went into the water. But oh my, how cold it was. The first dip of the summer is always cold, and running water never gets very warm. The children didn't stay too long, but Folke enjoyed splashing around in the brook. He didn't shiver at all.

"It's because I am so fat that I don't feel the cold," he said. "Eat properly, and your teeth won't chatter."

Afterwards they sat down among the forget-me-nots, and ate rolls with honey, and drank blackberry juice. It tasted delicious. The sun toasted their backs, the little birds sang in the hazel grove and in the water small fishes hurried by. The brook murmured and gurgled and everything was simply glorious. Now and then the cuckoo sounded its melodious call.

Folke cut each of them a hazel stick, peeling off the bark in a spiral, so the sticks looked as if they had been wrapped with white and brown ribbons. On the way home Pelle-Göran rode pickaback on Folke's shoulders, while Kaja picked flowers for grandmother.

"Don't you agree that the glen is fine?" asked Folke.

They willingly agreed to that.

"Say, Folke, why doesn't Ola Gädda like boys?" asked Pelle-Göran, from where he was hanging.

"Oh, so you have met Ola Gädda. Did he chase you away?"

"Not quite . . . but why, Folke?"

"Perhaps it is because he had bad luck with his own boy. But don't worry about that. Ola Gädda isn't mean, just a little stubborn and cross."

Pelle-Göran tried to find out more, but that was all Folke would say.

"Well, look at this, you are beginning to get color already, you little palefaces," said grandmother in delight, when they came home for dinner. She was pleased with their appetites, too. The macaroni pudding and the stewed fruit both slid down amazingly fast.

After dinner the children went out to the barn to play with the kittens and let the calves suck their fingers. Folke said they liked to do that. And then it was time to carry the food to Lubbe and Amelie. They sat quietly side by side and looked at the dog and the goose while they were eating, and not once did Amelie hiss at them. She was busy gulping down the oats and driving away the chickens who came running and wanted to taste. It was very clear that she considered the chickens plain trash, and felt herself vastly superior to them.

Afterwards Kaja and Pelle-Göran were allowed to go along and see how the cows were milked with the milking machine. And then Kaja planted her seventeen tulip bulbs along the east wall of the house. Folke helped her put them in the ground. Rosenose and Tigerpaw scratched along as well as they knew how. But, as Folke said, as gardeners they probably would not amount to much.

Soon came time to eat supper. They had porridge with

cinnamon and sugar, and hard roll sandwiches with cheese and smoked sausage, and it all tasted equally good.

They really ought to have gone to bed after that, for the sun had already set, and Pelle-Göran had yawned twice. But the nightingale began to sing in the glen, and the song was so beautiful that grandmother and Dela just stood there and listened with folded hands as though they were in church. So they all went out and sat down on "the oaken chairs," the garden furniture made of crooked oak branches, and there they sat for a long time. Nobody said a word. They only listened to the lovely sound.

"Well, you sang the cuckoo song nicely, Kaja, but you can't beat this one," said Folke when they could finally tear themselves loose and go in.

Soon the pale June moon rose over the forest, shining gently down on Stubba Farm, on all its people and all its animals.

Grandmother went straight off to bed as soon as she had said, "Goodnight, little Julius!" and spread a black cover over the cage of the parrot. Yawning widely, Folke listened to the weather report on the radio while he undressed. Dela turned in bed, wondering in her sleep where she might get a nice dress pattern for an eleven-year-old. And up in the gable room Pelle-Göran fell asleep with the black dachshund in one arm and the baby lion in the other. Kaja lay awake a while thinking about Rosenose. She sighed happily and said to herself that tomorrow she would write to Gertrud and tell about all these wonderful things down here on the South Ridge. Sleepily, she looked at the cloth rose standing right in the moonlight and looking almost like a real rose. If Gertrud only knew . . . but before she had time to think it out, she was sound asleep.

In the opening to the dog house stood Amelie, with the beak under her wing, and inside, with one eye open and ears alert, slept Lubbe, the caretaker of the farm. From the barn came the gentle noises of calves and kittens, and out into the night went the mother cat to hunt rats. In the field lay the cows and heifers chewing their cud. And from the glen rose the song of the nightingale mingling with the cool murmur of the brook.

7

The Pilferers

The days passed one after the other, and all equally pleasant for the children from the north. The wild strawberries ripened around Stubba Farm, and the children picked and ate.

Dela sewed not only one, but three new cotton dresses for Kaja; a red checkered one, a striped blue one and a yellow one with black dots. And Kaja looked like a different and much prettier girl when she put them on.

Sometimes, well, quite often really, Pelle-Göran thought about his Mamma. But he didn't worry so much about her any longer. He trusted the doctor, and he was sure Mamma was going to get well. Once in a while, though, he wondered if perhaps the doctor had spoken as he did just to keep him quiet. Then he became fussy about his food and difficult in other ways. But those times became less and less frequent. And to be absolutely certain, he already had

talked with grandmother about the spettecake. And grandmother had said she would be prepared for it. The day the
message came that his Mamma was well again and he could
go home, she would make a very fine spettecake. But he
would have to understand that an operation of that sort took
some time, so there was no hurry right now. And grandmother said she almost was glad about it, because she could
keep Pelle-Göran with her a while yet.

"I don't think we need to worry about the baking for the
doctor until the red whortleberries ripen and I have finished
making the jam," she said.

And grandmother's wise brown eyes and firm voice made
Pelle-Göran feel calm and secure. Soon she only needed to
look at him and he would know what was right and what
was wrong. People and animals obeyed her without grum-
bling, and Pelle-Göran was soon no exception.

He seldom was bored. He just didn't have time for that.
There was too much to do on Stubba Farm.

Folke was busy hoeing the potatoes. The spring had been
so late, there had been no time for that before. Grandmother and Dela also had much to do, so most of the time
the children had to take care of themselves. They helped a
little, dried the dishes, set the table, ran errands, cleaned the
parrot's cage and carried food to the "poultry," as grandmother called the chickens and the geese.

Every day Kaja locked herself in grandmother's room
and tried to teach Julius some new words. She was very
secretive about those little lessons. But she did say it looked
as if Julius didn't want to learn anything more.

"You just wait," said grandmother. "It takes a little time, but then you'll see it will go like a flash."

One day grandmother sent Kaja and Pelle-Göran to the village to do some shopping. They had been there before so they had no trouble finding it.

Close to the store they saw a laughing, shouting group of children crowded around something beside the stairs. When they got nearer they saw a little girl holding a rusty and well-worn bicycle, standing in the middle of the crowd. They were laughing at her. She was about eight or nine years old, and she looked around with angry, watchful eyes.

"Pilfer-lassie," laughed the boys, pretending to snatch the bicycle away from her. "Pilfer-lassie, pilfer-lassie!" shrilled the girls.

"Did she steal the bicycle?" asked Kaja, shocked.

"She sure did, or else it was that other pilferer, that brother of hers, who took it," grinned one of the taller boys.

"You are lying, William Nilsson," screamed the girl. "Stig got the bicycle from Oscar Persson when he helped with the hoeing of the potatoes. It was thrown away, it couldn't be used."

"Oh, that's what he says," laughed William Nilsson.

The girl stamped on the ground with her worn wooden shoes.

"You're all so mean I would like to spit at the whole lot of you," she cried.

"Oh, she is going to spit!" screamed the girls.

"There are bad people living up there on Klövatorp," said one girl importantly. "Everybody knows that your father stole things, Ellen."

"You can be bad people yourselves," shrilled the girl with the bicycle. "You are the meanest kids on all South Ridge, and you, William Nilsson, are the worst one of the lot."

William Nilsson grabbed the bicycle. "Watch out there, kid!" he said.

"Let go the bike. Let me alone, you hear! Or else you'll get it when Stig comes."

She bent down and picked up a stone.

66

"Now she'll throw stones at us," cried the children.

The door to the store opened.

"That pilfer-laddie is coming," somebody whispered, and the children quickly scattered in all directions.

A fair-haired boy, large and heavy, came out with a blue willow basket on his arm. He frowned as he looked at the children.

"Did they tease you?" he asked.

"Oh, they only yelled things and wanted to take the bicycle away from me," said the girl.

"Those two, also?" he asked, looking sideways at Kaja and Pelle-Göran.

"No, they are new, so they haven't started yet," said the girl indifferently.

The boy put the basket on the worn baggage carrier, lifted the girl up and pedalled off. Screeching, the old bicycle disappeared around the corner.

"Terrible," said Kaja. "I have never seen thieves before. Have you?"

"No," said Pelle-Göran. "Funny, though, they looked just like everybody else."

"I wonder what their father did," said Kaja. "It must have been something bad. Oh my, it is better not to have any Pappa. But it wasn't very nice the way they all ganged up on her. She was so little."

"Yes, but she was thinking about throwing stones," said Pelle-Göran.

"Yes, she did, of course, and she didn't look very nice."

Then they went into the store and bought everything on

67

grandmother's list. The storekeeper joked and chatted with them, offered them caramels and asked them how they liked South Ridge and if it were true that one of grandmother's cows had gotten twins. And they had such a good time in the store that they forgot what they had seen outside.

Perhaps they never would have thought about it again if they hadn't been reminded of it some weeks later.

Early one morning, just as they had gotten up, they heard Lubbe bark outside.

"It sounds like somebody coming," said grandmother. "Go and see who it is, please, and watch Lubbe."

A boy and a girl were hanging on the gate when they came out. Lubbe was jumping up and down, barking at them, and Amelie came waddling uneasily on her flat feet to watch the house and Lubbe.

Kaja pulled Pelle-Göran's arm.

"Look, the pilferers!" she whispered. "What do you think they want here?"

"You ask them," said Pelle-Göran, staying a few steps behind Kaja as she walked towards the gate.

"Keep still, Lubbe, go and lie down," said Kaja grasping the dog by the collar. "Hi there! What is it you want?" she called.

"Talk to Folke Bengtsson," said the fair-haired boy sullenly.

"Come in then, Lubbe isn't dangerous," said Kaja, pulling the dog aside.

She had to defend herself from Amelie, who couldn't

68

bear to see her friend being treated like this without coming over to nip her legs. The boy was about to open the gate, but the girl held him back, her little face screwed up as if she were ready to burst into tears.

"She's afraid of the dog. We'll wait here," said the boy.

Pelle-Göran rushed in to grandmother.

"Pilfer-lassie and pilfer-laddie are here, and they want to talk to Folke," he cried breathlessly.

Grandmother was standing at the stove. She turned around quickly.

"What did you say?" she said sternly. "Who are you giving such ugly names?"

"That was what William Nilsson and the others called them," Pelle-Göran defended himself.

"It was stupid and wrong for William Nilsson to do so. You must not repeat what someone like him says. And I certainly must have a talk with William Nilsson, if he goes around thinking up such silly things."

"What are their names then?" asked Pelle-Göran.

"If it is the children from Klövatorp you are talking about, their names are Stig and Ellen, so far as I know. Folke is out feeding the animals, but he'll soon be here. Ask the children to come in and get a little coffee in the meantime."

He ran back to them and said: "Grandmother wants Stig and Ellen to come in and get some coffee."

But not until grandmother herself came out and asked them in would they come. And they were not going to have any coffee. Oh no, they weren't hungry at all, and not thirsty either.

"How is your mother? Is her arm well now?" asked grandmother.

"No, her fingers are quite stiff. She can't do knitting any more," said the girl. "But Stig and I and . . ."

"Keep quiet, silly," her brother said, giving her a shove. "You are always babbling when grownups are talking."

"But she was asking," mumbled the girl.

"Tell her I'll come to see her as soon as I can," said grandmother.

The boy straightened up, and said that it wouldn't be necessary, because they were looking after her.

Then Folke came.

"Oh, there you are," he said. "I was just thinking about sending a message to Klövatorp asking you to come. I need help with the digging. And soon we'll begin cutting the grass, so you can begin today if you want."

Stig brightened. When he looked at Folke he didn't seem sullen at all.

"I'll just go home and tell mother," he said.

"You may sleep in the harness room here, so you won't have that long trip back and forth," said Folke.

"I have the bicycle, of course," said Stig gruffly.

But one could hear he was happy about the suggestion. It was decided that he should take his sister home and get the things he needed. Before they rode off grandmother succeeded in pressing upon them a bottle of liniment, a package of padding to wrap around the mother's ailing arm, and a bag with freshly baked bread. She said she wanted to know if their mother liked the bread, for after what she had heard she was an excellent baker.

"They say that her cinnamon bread is so very delicious," said grandmother. "Tell her I wonder what's the matter with these. I am not quite satisfied with them. Did I use too much cinnamon, maybe, or do I need some more sugar. Ask her about it!"

"Mother," said Folke, after the children from Klövatorp had left, "I've never heard anybody say there was some-

71

thing the matter with your cinnamon bread."

Grandmother smiled.

"It is always nice to find out how others do things," she said. "And the mother of these children used to be a baker in Astorp before they moved here last fall, so she must know how it ought to be."

"Where is their Pappa?" asked Pelle-Göran.

"Well, if we only knew that," sighed grandmother. "But now children, let us see that you are nice to Stig when he comes, do you hear?"

"How do you think Ola Gädda will take it, mother?" wondered Folke.

"He can say what he wants. This is good for him. Well, who knows! Maybe he'll soften in the end," said grandmother.

"You think so? I think he is a resentful old fool," said Folke, shaking his head.

Close to noon, perspiring and red, Stig came back on his screechy bicycle. His wooden shoes were tied together and slung over his shoulders, and the blue basket was on the baggage carrier. He disappeared into the harness room with his things, but returned quickly. Grandmother was sitting in the sun outside the kitchen door peeling potatoes. He walked over to her and said, "Mother says thanks for the salve for the arm, and says you could have had a little less butter, but she said that otherwise that bread of yours was real good."

Then off he clattered in his wooden shoes to join Folke

out in the field. Not once did he look at the children, who had decided to be friendly and who followed close on his heel, chatting and talking. He was a man now, going to work. He stayed with Folke, for Folke also was a man. That third man, little Pelle-Göran, felt he wasn't quite one of them, so he finally tired and trudged home again.

Ola Gädda was sharpening his axe on the grindstone beside the barn. He shaded his face with his hand and gazed towards Folke and Stig.

"I see we have strangers on the farm now," he said. "Then it be best to lock the door and keep the little we have."

"What kind of little?" asked Pelle-Göran curiously. "Do you have some little animals in there in your cottage, perhaps?"

"Animals? Oh yes, the spiders on the ceiling and the flies in the windows, they be my animals. I have no others any more," said the old man.

"What a pity! I've got a cat, a real living cat. He's called Tigerpaw. Say, if you'd let me turn that wheel, I'll let you borrow my cat sometime."

"What would I do with a cat?" said Ola Gädda absentmindedly, looking at the men in the field. "The kid looks as if he can go in there and do some work, for sure," he mumbled reluctantly.

Pelle-Göran turned the grindstone with both hands. He was happy, for finally he was doing a man's work.

"I can bring Tigerpaw as soon as he has had his milk," he said.

The old man tried the newly sharpened edge of the axe with his thumb, saying there was no use bringing him a cat, for cats were just like people. As long as they were small, they were all right, but later on they all turned into "good-for-nothings."

"Cats oughtn't to be born, and no human being either," he said turning his back to the boy.

Sadly, Pelle-Göran walked home. He had become attached to Ola Gädda, and wanted very much to make him happy. But what could he do with somebody who didn't even like cats?

When they ate supper Stig sat silently beside Folke. Grandmother put his food on his plate, as she did for Kaja and Pelle-Göran. He ate with good appetite but seldom looked up from his plate. When they left the table he quietly thanked grandmother and Folke for the food.

"Would you like to go down to the brook for a while with Pelle-Göran and me?" asked Kaja shyly.

Stig shook his head and disappeared into the harness room. He did not come out all evening.

He continued to be silent and unsociable. Every evening he locked himself in the harness room or else he mounted his bicycle and rattled home to Klövatorp not to return until the next morning.

"He works hard," said Folke, "and he needs plenty of sleep. Just leave him in peace, since he doesn't want company."

The weather was hot now, so boiling hot in the sun that the children didn't often go out into the open field. They

74

preferred the shady glen for swimming and playing with their small boats in the brook. Dela taught Kaja to make some kind of long canoes out of white paper. They dropped them into the water and let them drift with the current. They had a whole fleet and had exciting races with them.

Sometimes Folke would wade into the brook and stalk the salmon trout among the boulders. He grasped the struggling fish behind the gills and tossed it up on the shore. Grandmother was always glad when he came home with fish.

But later on when the clover was in bloom and its sweet fragrance hung over the fields, and bumble bees and honey bees were at their busiest, came time to get the hay in all over South Ridge. The two horses on Stubba Farm had been enjoying lazy days out on pasture. They were mostly used to cart lumber and wood in the forest during winter-time. But when haying time came they had to come along. They were needed then.

Everybody on the farm took part in the haying, even grandmother and Dela. Ola Gädda left his woodpile and picked up the rake instead. He and Stig worked side by side, but not a word did they say to one another.

Kaja and Pelle-Göran loved the haying, especially when they were allowed to ride on the top of the load and jump around in the fresh new hay in the hayloft. At meals they appeared with straw in their hair, but nobody had time to pay attention to that on busy days like these. Both of them had a good tan, and a ravenous appetite. Folke became thinner during the heat but the children's cheeks grew rounder.

8

A Night in the Barn

One morning some time after Stig had arrived on the farm, grandmother remarked rather thoughtfully at the breakfast table, "I can't understand what's happened to the chickens to make them stop laying eggs in the middle of the summer. Yesterday there weren't more than four eggs in the nests, today only six. Eat your omelets now, children, for if this is going to go on, you won't have another one for a long time."

Grandmother's omelet was wonderful. She made it in a huge pan on the top of the stove. It was golden and juicy, and filled with delicious pieces of smoked bacon. She shook the pan and poked the thick batter with a thin, flexible knife while it was baking. Oh, how good it smelled! The children, standing beside her and smacking their lips, looked at her with tense eyes as she turned it on a lid. For a lot of eggs went into it, that was sure. And if the chickens stopped lay-

ing eggs there wouldn't be any more omelets. Not a spettecake, either, thought Pelle-Göran, alarmed.

"No, this can't be right," said grandmother again a few
days later. Can it be that the chickens are laying their eggs
outside somewhere? Three eggs I got today from my
twenty-four chicks. You'll have to search the barn, children. Perhaps they are laying the eggs in the hay."

Ola Gädda heard about it when he came to get his daily
milk ration. He looked straight at grandmother, and said:

"So, it's beginning now," he said glumly.

"What do you mean, Ola?" said grandmother surprised.

"So, ye're eggs are going?" said Ola. "Strange. How
come? Couldn't be ye've had thieves here, could it?"

"Oh, nonsense," said grandmother a little impatiently.

"Well, ye just remember I don't want anything to do
with this," said Ola Gädda and left.

Kaja gave Pelle-Göran a push and pulled him outside
with her.

"What do you think he meant?" she whispered. "Do you
think he means Stig?"

Pelle-Göran thought that was what he meant.

"It's only because he can't stand boys," he said. "What
would Stig do with so many eggs?"

"Oh, he could, of course take them home to Klövatorp,"
said Kaja. "Grandmother says they are having a hard time
there. But I don't think he did it."

"Nor do I. I think Stig is nice. Ola Gädda is an old dumbbell."

"But it is true that it started only after Stig came here, and

78

grandmother began leaving the door to the chicken house open because of the heat. And the basket, Pelle-Göran. He always takes the basket with him when he rides home."

"Do you mean that he snitches eggs and takes them with him in the basket?"

"I don't know," said Kaja reluctantly. "But he *could* do it if he wanted to. And that's what Ola Gädda thinks."

"What are we going to do? Can we ask grandmother? Or Folke, perhaps?"

"Yes, but it would be terrible if he hadn't done it. No, I know. We'll sneak into the harness room and see if he has any eggs in that basket."

"Yes, that's what we can do. Let's do it now when he is out. Come on! Hurry!"

They crept into the stable and opened the unlocked door to the harness room. First they didn't see any basket, but finally they discovered it pushed in under the bed. Kaja pulled the little pin out of the loop and opened the lid.

There were no eggs. There were two big grey balls of woolen yarn and something more.

Knitting!

"A half-finished stocking," said Kaja amazed. "Thick woolen socks. And a finished stocking. Look, such a big foot it has. That's funny. What's he going to use it for?"

"Put it back! He is coming!" whispered Pelle-Göran.

They barely had time to push the basket under the bed before the door opened. But it wasn't Stig. It was Ola Gädda who stood there. He looked at them queerly.

"Oh, so ye're looking for eggs here," he said sternly.

"We . . . we weren't looking for anything," stammered Kaja.

"There are no eggs here," said Pelle-Göran. "There are only stockings in the basket."

"I don't think that Stig is stealing," said Kaja.

But as she said it she was wondering if it might not be so after all.

"Usch!" said Pelle-Göran. "If Stig is stealing I am going to be very unhappy. I like Stig."

"The father was a thief," said Ola Gädda darkly. "When the cat is spotted, the kittens have dark streaks."

"They are not always that way," said Kaja. "Mirran is spotted, but she had a coal black kitten and a silver grey one."

"Hm," said Ola Gädda. "But who's taken the eggs then?"

"We'll do some spying and be sure to find out," said Pelle-Göran fiercely.

But none of them could think of how to do that. The

barn had been thoroughly searched, and also all possible places outside where the chickens might have gone to lay their eggs.

At the dinner table the talk turned to the eggs again.

"There's of course no chance that somebody might have been here and stolen them," said Folke.

At this they all noticed that Stig turned a deep red. Both children saw it. Grandmother saw it, too. She looked thoughtfully at Stig, as if the thought had struck her, "Could it be he, after all?"

"No," continued Folke, "if we had a thief here, Lubbe, of course, would have sounded the alarm. I'm sure we'll suddenly find all the eggs under some bushes. We know how crazy chickens can be. Kaja and Pelle-Göran, who have plenty of time, will have to shadow those chickens and see where they go."

"Don't they lay eggs during the night?" wondered Kaja.

Grandmother said, both at day and at night. But she said it absent-mindedly, as if she were thinking about something entirely different. Stig was sitting there pecking at his fried herring with his fork, but forgetting to eat. It was as if he suddenly had shrunk and become much smaller.

"Chicken detectives, go to it!" said Pelle-Göran. "I'll sneak up behind each chick, and grab the egg as soon as she lays it."

"You do that, but don't chase my biddies," said grandmother. "You'll get ten öre for each egg you find."

Grandmother removed Stig's plate without saying a word about all the food left on it. She served the rhubarb dessert and cream and then she said: "I am wondering if there isn't thunder in the air. It is so close that even Lubbe has lost his appetite. When he does that he usually expects bad weather."

"We'll see if we can't get in the last of the hay," said Folke, standing up.

Yes, it was close. All during the night the windows and doors were open everywhere, and still people turned and twisted in their beds without being able to sleep. Lubbe lay panting outside his house and most of the time Amelie stayed down in the pond with the other geese. The cows waded in the brook up to their bellies and stood there for hours. One night Folke slept in the hammock under the apple trees.

Pelle-Göran and Kaja shadowed the chickens. As soon as they saw one wander off by herself they were after her. But her errand always seemed to be something like scratching for worms or taking a sand bath in the yard. Then they went into the chicken coop and examined the nests, while the hens fluttered around and the feathers flew. Triumphantly they came out with two eggs and received ten öre each from grandmother. In the afternoon they found three more eggs. But that was all for that day.

"What can we do?" asked Pelle-Göran in the evening.

"We'll have to keep watch tonight," said Kaja. "We can stay in the hayloft where we can peek down at the hens through the openings. And if a thief comes, we'll run in and wake up Folke."

"Do you think that grandmother will let us?"

"We'll sneak into the barn after grandmother and Folke have gone to bed."

"Well . . . but what if the thief gets hold of us and does something bad to us. We should have somebody big with us. Maybe Ola Gädda."

"Oh no," said Kaja. "Ola Gädda is so sure that it is Stig, he would only laugh at us. No, I know now! Stig, of course. He is so strong that no thief would dare to take him on. Come on!"

A small ladder was standing near the little opening under the roof which was supposed to be the window in the harness room. Kaja climbed up and peeked in. Pelle-Göran followed. The kerosene lamp was lighted and they could see Stig stretched out across the bed. It looked as if his shoulders were shaking.

"Is he crying?" whispered Pelle-Göran.

"Yes," whispered Kaja. "Poor Stig."

Then they saw him get up. He rubbed his eyes with the back of his hands, and then he pulled the blue basket out from under the bed. He took up the stocking with the knitting needles in, then sat down on the side of the bed and began to knit.

The children were so surprised they almost rolled down the ladder. A boy who was knitting! And not only that. The rough hands of the boy were knitting as if they never had done anything else. His fingers flew, the needles flashed in the lamp light and the grey woolen ball of yarn whirled around. Neither grandmother nor Dela could knit faster than Stig from Klövatorp.

83

So that was what he did every evening!

"Come, let's get down," whispered Kaja.

"Aren't you going to knock and ask him?" whispered Pelle-Göran.

"Not now," said Kaja.

But just before they could get down, Stig happened to look at the window. He jumped up, threw the knitting under the bed and ran over to the window.

"Is somebody there?"

And before they got down the ladder he was outside the door.

"Oh, so you're out here spying!" he cried and he sounded so angry they didn't dare to speak.

"What did you think you would see?" he asked scornfully. "Did you think you would see eggs, maybe?"

"Oh no," said Pelle-Göran, "don't get mad at us because we peeked."

"Please, Stig," said Kaja, "we wanted to ask you to help us catch the thief tonight."

"Oh, sure, you want me to believe that. The thief, that's me, you know. Aren't you all thinking that? And why didn't you come to the door? What's the idea of climbing the ladder?"

"Because it is more fun to climb ladders," said Kaja frankly. "And just wait now, till you hear."

"Wait yourself," said Stig. "Tell me what you saw when you were peeking into the harness room."

"We only saw you were sad," said Kaja quietly.

"Oho," said Stig. "You were wrong then. Don't you see how happy I am," he said, starting to laugh, but it did not sound like real laughter.

"We saw you knitting stockings too," said Pelle-Göran.

At first Stig didn't answer. But after a while he said: "And now I suppose you're going to blab about it all over South Ridge?"

"We aren't tattletales," said Kaja, indignantly.

"Noho, we sure aren't," said Pelle-Göran.

85

"It's nobody's business but yours. You knit as much as you like, if you think it is fun," said Kaja.

"I don't think it is fun," said Stig curtly. "Now, what did you want with me?"

Quickly Kaja told of how they had thought of staying in the barn to wait for the egg thief.

"He must be coming at night, of course, since there always is someone around here in the daytime," she said. "And we are afraid he might do something to us if we are alone, so that's why we want you to be with us."

Stig looked straight at them.

"Yes, but haven't you seen that everybody thinks I am the one who is stealing the eggs?" he said slowly.

"We don't," said Kaja and Pelle-Göran.

"Are you sure about that?"

Both of them said they were sure.

"We can shake hands and look you straight in the eyes to show you," said Pelle-Göran.

So they shook hands and looked earnestly into his eyes.

"Well," said Stig, sounding a little more friendly now, "of course I can lie in the hay tonight, if that's what you want. And I also would like to find out where those eggs go."

That evening grandmother didn't have to urge them to go to bed. When she came to say good night they were lying nicely in their beds with the blankets all the way up to the chin. Grandmother had no idea that they had all their clothes on. Folke had gone to town on his bicycle and had taken Lubbe with him so he could get some exercise. But

86

grandmother, who was always sleepy at night went to bed. They could hear through the floor how she wound the clock, how she splashed in the water and how she chatted with Julius. And then the house grew quiet.

"Should we wait until Folke's back?" whispered Pelle-Göran.

"No, he might be gone for hours," answered Kaja. "Suppose we should fall asleep. We'd better sneak out now."

They tiptoed down and climbed cautiously out of the low window in the big room. They might just as well have gone out through the door, which stood open as usual for the sake of coolness. But it seemed more exciting to sneak through the window. They landed among peonies and monkshoods in the flower bed along the wall. Like two little rats they scurried across the yard to the barn. The gravel was still lukewarm under their bare feet. Over by the dog house Amelie wakened and stretched her neck. But she immediately recognized them and stuck her bill under her wing again, as they disappeared through the barn door.

Stig was not yet there.

"Maybe he went to sleep and forgot all about it," said Pelle-Göran.

"He'll come," said Kaja.

Near the wall to the chicken coop they each dug a hole in the hay. Through the cracks they barely glimpsed the chickens in the dim light. Some slept on their perches, others still stayed in their nests. In one corner stood a cage with little chicks, and from there they heard little peeps once in a while.

The door to the chicken house consisted of two shutters, one above the other. The upper one stood wide open. With a watchdog like Lubbe, and not to speak of Amelie, a few yards away, there was, of course, no danger that a fox or a badger could sneak in.

The hay smelled sweetly of clover. There was a gentle rustle when they stirred. Somewhere under the floor of the barn the rats were gnawing.

"Why doesn't he come?" sighed Pelle-Göran impatiently.

"Sh-h," said Kaja. "What was that?"

The lock on the gate clicked and the gravel on the road crunched. Folke came riding in on his bicycle and Lubbe puffed past the barn over to Amelie. They heard Folke put aside the bicycle and fill Lubbe's dish with water from the pump. Lubbe gulped and drank and Folke disappeared into the house. A little while after, Stig came padding along.

"We thought you'd never come," whispered Kaja. "Look, we have made a hole for you beside us. You'll never believe how soft it is lying here."

"And now you think we are going to catch the thief," said Stig, crawling down into the hollow.

"Yes, because I am sure we can both see and hear if someone should sneak into the chicken house," said Kaja.

They lay silent for a while. Pelle-Göran yawned widely, but he wouldn't admit that he was sleepy.

"Just think if grandmother knew we were here," he said giggling.

Kaja pinched him and whispered that he must be quiet, so the thief wouldn't hear him if he came.

"The thieves won't be out this early," said Stig. "They won't come before they're sure everybody is asleep."

"Then we can chat a little, sort of quietly," said Kaja. "Do you go to school, Stig? In the winter, I mean."

"Yes. I am going next year, too," he answered.

But he didn't sound very happy about it.

"What do you want to be when you get big?" asked Pelle-Göran. "I want to be a fire chief."

"I like farm work best but I suppose I'll have to go to sea," said Stig and sighed.

"Why?" asked Kaja.

"Oh, to get away from silly people," said Stig.

"Say Stig, why do you knit stockings if you don't like it?"

"Because mother has pains and can't do it."

"Who gets those stockings then?"

"We leave them at the store. We owe the storekeeper money so we leave the stockings instead. They are good stockings. The storekeeper sells them to stores in Landskrona and Hälsingborg. People use them in their boots in winter time, people who work outdoors. All three girls at home are knitting, too."

"How many brothers and sisters do you have?"

"Six."

"You are lucky, you! I don't have any."

"But you have Pelle-Göran," said Stig surprised.

89

"No, we are only cousins," yawned Pelle-Göran. "Where is your Pappa now?"

"At sea. We haven't heard from him since last fall when he brought us here, and left us with grandfather."

"Do you have a grandfather, too?" said Kaja wistfully.

"Yes, you know that. Ola Gädda. But he won't have anything to do with us because he is mad at father. When we came to Klövatorp, he moved here to the little cottage."

"Ola Gädda!" burst out both children in amazement. "Is he your grandfather?"

"Yes, though he is ashamed of it. He left the cow and the pig there and came here, even if Klövatorp was his own place. He said . . ."

Stig suddenly stopped.

"What then, Stig?"

"That all his life he'd been honest, and that he wouldn't live together with a pack of thieves."

"That's awful," said Kaja, shocked. "And what did your Pappa say then?"

"He said that you might have forgiven that old miserable thing, father, and now I haven't any place to leave wife and children since she got that ache and can't do any more baking. I'm aiming to go to sea and earn money so we can live, all of us, but I thought, though, that these poor things might get a roof over their heads with you while I'm gone. And then grandfather said, 'Ye can stay here, but I'm going.' And he hasn't said a word to any of us since. And not a word have we heard from father, either. But we are used to that. Once he was gone for two years. But we managed as long as mother could work. Oh, we'll do all right now, too, don't worry."

"Stig," said Kaja in a low voice, "what did your Pappa do that made your grandfather so mad at him?"

"Well, when he was eighteen years old he took a spoon hook from a farmer in Magleröd," said Stig, in a half-choked voice.

"A spoon hook, what's that?"

"It's something they used to fish with some time ago. It's shiny. It's something like they use for trolling. It sure isn't something that costs a lot of money. But theft is theft, and grandfather, he never can forget it. And father, he can never forget that grandfather beat him with an oak stick when he found out about it. That's why he left home, and he hadn't been back home before last fall when he had to come."

"I think Ola Gädda is mean," said Kaja.

"Ola Gädda is a *tiny* bit nice, too," objected Pelle-Göran.

And just as he was saying that, he fell asleep.

He woke up several times, one time because a straw pricked his ear, another time because one of his legs had gone to sleep. Next he had to sneeze because his nose was filled with hayseeds.

But the fourth time he jumped up, because Stig had grasped his arm roughly, and the rooster sent out his first "cock-a-doodle-do" from inside the chicken house. The early light of the morning was streaming in through the openings in the barn and the swallows under the eaves had begun their twittering.

"Sh-h," whispered Stig. "The thief is here."

He and Kaja were lying with their noses close to the boards, peeking through the openings. Pelle-Göran shivered with excitement and put one eye to a knothole. His heart began to hammer. It was frightening. A dark head appeared above the closed shutter. Pelle-Göran's eyes were so filled with sleep that at first he could not see who it was. He blinked his eyes and stared, and then he heard Kaja excitedly draw in her breath.

Then he saw. But oh! It was only Lubbe who came jumping over, steering straight for the nests.

Pelle-Göran was just about to burst out laughing when

Stig's hand squeezed his shoulder hard and meaningly. Then he saw something strange. The dog rose on his hind legs and stretched its tousled head into one of the nests. A moment later he turned and walked carefully towards the door, carrying something white between his teeth. Behind him cackled the stirred-up hens. Cautiously, like an Indian on the warpath, he hoisted himself up on the shutter, balancing for a moment, then ever so gently and carefully, he jumped down.

The children looked amazed at one another. Lubbe! It was Lubbe who was the egg thief!

Stig jumped up.

"Hurry," he whispered. "We'll have to see where he goes."

They scrambled up, shivering and sleepy-eyed, and hurried out, catching a glimpse of the dog's tail as it disappeared around the corner. When they reached the corner they saw that he, still with the egg between his teeth, was walking towards the refuse pile, where he vanished among the "pesky nettles," as grandmother called the tall thicket of nettles.

They didn't have time to think about the fact that nettles burn, before they were right in the midst of them. And there stood the old glutton, lapping up the contents of a newly broken egg. They startled him when they came rushing up, but he was still licking his mouth, when, slightly taken aback, he trotted away. The ground in the nettle thicket was completely covered with egg shells.

93

"What a scamp," said Kaja, overwhelmed.

"What do you think grandmother will say?" cried Pelle-Göran.

"Ya, I wouldn't like to be Lubbe now," said Stig.

The nettle blisters burned on their bare legs when they ran back again, and they almost fell over Amelie who was on her way down to the pond to take her morning dip. Lubbe had crawled in behind the dog house and was looking guiltily out, when they came running past.

As if they had wings, Kaja and Pelle-Göran flew in to wake grandmother. They didn't need to. She already was standing in front of the kitchen stove in her housecoat and with her night braid down her back.

"Grandmother!" cried Pelle-Göran, "we've found the thief, grandmother! Ouch, my legs are hurting."

"How you scared me, children," wailed grandmother.

"You are up already? And what is it you are saying—which thief?"

"The egg thief, of course," laughed Kaja.

And then, with many screams and much laughter, they told all about it, while grandmother put lime liniment on the nettle blisters. Meanwhile Folke came out from his room and then there was even more laughter and noise.

"Lubbe, that rascal!" said Folke. "Well, that's really something!"

"No wonder he couldn't eat his food after having feasted on all my eggs," said grandmother. "Such a sly thing. Of course, once in a while he has helped himself to one or two cookies. And once he ran away with a package of liver sausage I had put down. And he's always been crazy about eggs. But I never thought he would break into the chicken coop. What are we going to do with him, Folke?"

Folke took an egg and walked out to Lubbe. He put it on the ground in front of him and said: "Yes, eggs are wonderful, dear Lubbe, but they are not for you. And here at Stubba Farm we don't want a dog who steals. Shame on you, old Lubbe. And now I'll have to punish you or else you will go and do it again."

He broke off a willow branch and gave the dog a few light raps. Lubbe howled and wailed, although on his thick fur it couldn't possibly have hurt very much. He howled because he felt ashamed. But the faithful Amelie came dashing up from the pond when she heard her friend's wailing. Hissing and quacking she flew right at Folke, nipping him again and again. And then she placed herself in front of the crestfallen Lubbe, flapping her outspread white wings, sprinkling drops of water all around her, "Come here, if you dare!" They laughed until they cried at the brave old goose. Kaja ran in to get a carrot for her, for there was nothing she liked as well as carrots.

"What be all this noise so early in the morning?" muttered Ola Gädda, coming around the corner.

"We have caught the egg thief!" screamed Pelle-Göran.

And then they told Ola Gädda about the night in the barn, and how Lubbe had come sneaking with the egg. At first the old man looked doubtful. But later on when they all went over to the nettle grove, and saw the pile of egg shells, he said that he had, of course, heard that dogs did like eggs, but who would have thought that of Lubbe, who got almost everything he wanted anyway?

But on the ladder outside the harness room sat Stig smiling in the morning sunshine. Nobody had seen him so happy before.

"Well, hm," said Ola Gädda to Folke, "can ye lend me the laddies to stack up firewood today?"

"The laddies," he said. Pelle-Göran jumped for joy. Because there were only two laddies there, he and Stig!

"Yes, that'll be all right," said Folke. "But I'll need Stig again in the afternoon."

"I don't think Lubbe will go into the chicken house very soon after this," said Kaja.

"I don't think so either," said grandmother. "But we had better be safe than sure, and lock the chickens in for the night after this. I can just imagine how many trips he has made over to the nettles every morning."

Kaja had already gone out to the nests and had found eleven eggs.

"Today it will be omelet for breakfast," said grandmother. "And now come in and we'll all have a sip of coffee. Then I think you children will have to go to bed. I don't suppose you had much sleep last night."

"Oh yes, we did and Pelle-Göran snored," said Kaja.

Grandmother cut some white bread and spread it with honey for the children. Stig got two pieces, with an extra large helping of honey. They all understood why.

Later on, Pelle-Göran learned to put up a real Skanish woodpile, one that is round and tall and pointed and looks almost like a beehive for giant bees. It was a special art, and he was very proud that he was learning it.

Ola Gädda didn't say much while they stacked the wood,

only, "It be three piles for sure, this here," or, "there be wood the winter through, here." And Stig was silent, too. But when Folke came later and called Stig, the old man said: "Thanks for letting me have 'im. The lad works well."

After Folke and Stig had left, Pelle-Göran said, "Stig is very clever, he can knit stockings, too."

Ola Gädda didn't believe that, so Pelle-Göran told all about the knitting of the stockings and the storekeeper and the mother's stiff fingers. First, when he told it all he remembered he wasn't supposed to be a tattletale, and he was a little ashamed of himself. But Ola Gädda stood staring down at his wooden shoes. He did not look very happy.

9
Mons the Thatcher

"Mother, have you seen how those cats have damaged the roof on the barn?" said Folke one day. "They are playing up there, and they don't bother about going down when they want to scratch. They think straw is just as good to scratch in as sand. They have made a large hole, and if it starts raining now, the rain will go straight through into the stalls."

"But how could that have happened?" said grandmother. "How do they get up there? There is no ladder."

"I think they must have climbed up on the grindstone down there, and from there up on the roof. I have moved it away now, but the damage is already done."

"Oh well, the straw was old and rotten, and the roof was going to be fixed this fall anyway. We shall have to send for Mons the Thatcher," said grandmother, after she had seen the damage to the barn roof.

"Well, children," said Folke, "if you like stories, be sure

to be there then. There is nobody on the whole Ridge who is so full of stories as Mons the Thatcher."

"Yes, he is a clever man," said grandmother. "He was supposed to be a teacher, but he became ill and had to stay in bed for several years. That's probably where he thought up all those stories. And later on, when he became well again, he thought he was too old to go to school. He said it was a healthier life to stay outdoors and fix roofs, and that's what he has been doing ever since."

A few days later Mons the Thatcher arrived. He was a tall, large-boned fellow with a well-worn broad brimmed hat pushed way back on his head. He laughed heartily when he saw the dark spot where the straw had been ripped up.

"Well, you see, the cats and I are old partners," he said. "I have talked to them and they have promised to get me work. And this shows that they are keeping their promise. I'll tell you, the cats on South Ridge have made many old straw roofs ready for me."

He took off his hat and made a deep bow in the direction of the barnyard cats, both of whom were watching their children playing in the yard.

"Thank you my friends, this was well done," he said.

Pelle-Göran looked from Mons to the cats, and then from the cats to Mons again. Could this be true? Could that fellow really talk with the cats?

He crept close to grandmother and in a whisper he asked her how this could happen. But even though he whispered ever so lightly, Mons the Thatcher heard him.

"Oh yes, all the old thatchers know the cat language," he said winking slyly.

"The dog language, too?" asked Pelle-Göran.

"No, I think mother Klara knows that better than I do," said Mons, putting the ladder up against the eaves.

"Grandmother," said Pelle-Göran, "do you know the dog language?"

"Oh yes, old Lubbe and I understand one another very well," she said.

"Yes, but what's it like when you talk it? Do you yell?"

"Ladies don't yell," said Mons, climbing up on the roof on all fours. "Well, well, there's quite a lot we have to tear out and repair here. It's a good thing I asked Oskar Persson to put aside some straw until fall for this thing. That is, I mean, after I had talked to the cats."

"Oh phooey!" said Pelle-Göran. "You are only fooling. I don't believe cats and dogs can talk."

"There is something to that, though," said grandmother.

"Some day you'll hear it yourself," said Mons, and sat down across the top of the roof. Then he began to tear away straw, throwing it down so fast it whirled around their ears, and they had to move away. Grandmother went in.

"I'm sure there must be a cat language," said Kaja. "Haven't you seen how Mirran and her kittens talk together. 'Ki-i-ttens,' she mews when she doesn't see them. 'Ye-ee-e,' mew the kittens and come running. 'M-y-y, how dirr-ty you are,' she scolds them, and licks them clean. 'Oh-h, so ni-ice,' purrs one kitten, 'Mi-i-ilk,' mews another searching for a nipple and beginning to drink. Yes, if you really try to listen you may hear all that."

"That girl she knows about it, that's for sure," said Mons the Thatcher from the roof. "But not everyone has his ears along."

When nobody was looking Pelle-Göran just had to feel if his ears were there. Oh yes, he did have them with him. They were fastened, of course. He walked over to Mirran and the kittens and tried to listen to them, but they weren't saying anything just then, only hunting butterflies in the grass.

After a while he tired of it. But he had one of his inquisitive days, so he went back to the thatcher and asked him why he had to get straw from Oskar Persson when they themselves had a big stack outside the barn. Then, he found out that Folke had threshed his straw with the machine, and that one got much stronger and better thatch from hand-threshed straw. There weren't many people who threshed by hand nowadays, so if one wanted fine roof straw one had to order a long time ahead.

"Soon we won't find anyone who will thresh the old way and then it's going to be hard to keep up the old roofs, and I don't suppose they'll be making new thatched roofs at all," he said.

"What will you do then, Mr. Thatcher?" asked Pelle-Göran.

"I think I'll be a fine gentleman and lie on my back looking at the sun," said Mons the Thatcher, laughing, with his head thrown back so that his silver grey stub of a beard glittered in the light.

"Maybe you could start a circus and talk with the cats," said Pelle-Göran. "I think there would be many who would come and listen to that, and then you would earn lots of money."

"I'll think it over," said Mons the Thatcher seriously. "But I'm not so sure I can get the cats with me on that. They're kind of shy."

Folke hitched up the horses and drove off to get the straw. Pelle-Göran and Kaja wanted to go along, but grandmother said, "No, as soon as I finish baking, I want you two to go along with me to the clogmaker, so he can take your measurements. Go and get Mons the Thatcher so he can get a sip of coffee. And you two will have some fruit juice, I suppose?"

When the children returned with the thatcher, grandmother brought out a tray and put it on the garden table.

"Mons, you can do with a little rest, I think," she said.

"Sit down there in the shade and chat a little with the children while I finish my baking. I have bread in the oven, so I have to stay inside with my coffee cup. But if Mons should happen to tell something nice, I think I'll hear it through the window."

"Thank you," said Mons and sat down on the oak bench.

Grandmother poured the coffee, put the pitcher with juice on the table and went in. She had given them a whole mountain of shiny fresh sweet rolls and fragrant cookies, and the cherry juice was cellar cool and wonderful. No matter how many glasses they drank, they could still drink more.

"Oh, how nice this is," sighed Kaja. "Why do we have to go to that old cloakmaker? I wish we could sit here and listen to stories all day long."

"Grandmother said we were going there to be measured for cloaks," said Pelle-Göran puzzled. "But what'll I do with a cloak? I've no use for such things."

Mons the Thatcher dipped a roll in his coffee and ate the soft roll with enjoyment.

"Oh, so you are going to the clogmaker? Haven't you ever been there?"

"No. Did she say 'clog'—well, that's different!"

"I should say so. Clogs are the same as wooden shoes. Some people call the clogmaker a cobbler, or even a cobblemaker."

"Wooden shoes," said Pelle-Göran. "Then we'll get wooden shoes, you and I, Kaja. That'll be fun."

"Lots of fun," said Kaja.

"Oh sure," said Mons. "The clogmaker is a good one. He measures so well and tries your clogs on so carefully that they fit your feet like the softest leather shoes. Everybody working in the field has wooden shoes, for leather shoes wouldn't do there."

"Folke, too! And Ola Gädda and Stig," said Pelle-Göran.

"I don't," said Mons, "they are no good on a roof. But most of the time children in the countryside run around in wooden shoes to save the leather ones. I am sure you have seen that. But now there are machine-made wooden shoes to be brought at Epa in Landskrona and Hälsingborg and everywhere, anyway. So the good old clogmaker work will soon go the way of the thatchers and the thatched roofs. But if you still care to listen I can tell you a story about a clog-maker who changed his profession."

"Please, tell!" begged Kaja.

"Why did he change his p'hfession?" asked Pelle-Göran with his mouth full of cookies.

"Why? Well, because of a little mistake, just like when you mixed up clog and cloak. By the way, little lassie, you have traveled around so much, have you ever been to Kivik?"

"Kivik, oh, yes, that's where they have the fair."

"Sure. Well, then you may have seen the house where he lived. I mean that old low whitewashed one, where the climbing roses grow all the way up, even over the roof. That little one standing in a grove of hazel bushes, at the crossroad just outside the place. Remember?"

Kaja wrinkled her brow and tried to think.

"Yes, I think I almost . . ." she said a little vaguely.

"Over the door hangs a rusty old sign on a curlicue of wrought iron. It is shaped like a big heart, just like the heart of a waffle, with squares in it, and the climbing roses have grown all around it. If you push the roses aside a little, ever so carefully, you might see a verse which is printed with old-fashioned letters. This is what it says:

"In this abode dwelleth Frans the wafflebaker,
Who in his younger days was known as cobblemaker.
For Love's own Sake, he stoppeth carving Shoes
And maketh of the Lady's Waffles better Use."

"Yes, that Frans, the cobbler who built the house, was a young and clever fellow with happy, lively eyes. At the market in Kivik he set up a booth where he sold his clogs and took orders for new ones. One market day it happened that among all those people, he met a girl he never had seen before. Her name was Pernilla, Paul's daughter. And she came from that part of Skane, where people say the most beautiful girls live. Well, I don't mean to brag about it by mentioning the place, but she was called The Rose of South Ridge, so you'll understand she wasn't exactly ugly.

The girl's father was called Paul Swensson and he was with her at the market. He wanted to buy a couple of young horses there. But they also had another errand. A wealthy farmer by the name of Jöns Oredsson had proposed to Pernilla. His farm wasn't more than three quarters of a mile from Kivik. And Pernilla and her father had been invited there so they could see how well she would live if she said yes to Jöns Oredsson. They had been there and had seen the fine house and the rich belongings, and Pernilla's father had nothing against getting Jöns for a son-in-law. Pernilla herself didn't think there was anything the matter with the farm but Jöns was big and fat and had a stomach like a bass drum. And his eyes were bleary, and he had a fierce temper. So Pernilla had asked if she might think it over a while and decide before evening.

And now she was walking there between the father and the suitor, worrying about what to answer. People were milling around them, screaming and laughing, the hand organs were shrilling and the German with the puppet theatre rang his bell. And there came Frans towards Pernilla. And believe me, he looked at her. He tore off his cap and threw it high up in the air, he felt that happy. And Pernilla, well, she looked at Frans, turning red and white, and thinking that if Jöns Oredsson had been like him and had had such happy and lively eyes, well, then she would have known what to answer. So there they stood, Frans and Pernilla, just looking at one another.

When Jöns Oredsson discovered what was going on he became worried and angry. It really did not look good that the girl to whom he had proposed should be standing there looking as if she were dreaming beautiful dreams, because such a good-for-nothing was looking at her. He knew very well who Frans was, because he had ordered many a pair of wooden shoes for his servants from him.

"Move on, cobblemaker, you are blocking the way for the Rose of South Ridge and her father," he said gruffly,

sticking out his fat stomach across which a heavy gold chain glittered.

Many a time, of course, Frans had heard about The Rose of South Ridge and all her suitors. Sadly he moved aside. There was nothing else to do, he thought, for a poor clog-maker would certainly not have a chance with her.

But Pernilla just stood there, not taking her lovely eyes off Frans. The hand organs shrilled and the noise from the market people was so loud that she didn't quite hear what Jöns Oredsson said. She thought he had called Frans a wafflebaker.

"Father, dear," she said, pulling her father's arm. "I have decided to say no to Jöns Oredsson. I only want to marry a wafflebaker."

The father and Jöns Oredsson were completely upset. What kind of nonsense was this? The father told her not to joke about serious things. And Jöns Oredson said that she would be sadly mistaken if she were thinking about getting a man like Jöns Oredsson to bake waffles. But he said that if she were so fond of waffles, she only had to remember that if she married him, Jöns Oredsson, she would be getting seven maids who might bake waffles and spettecake all day long.

But then swore Pernilla that if she could not have a waffle-baker, marriage would not be for her.

Jöns Oredsson was furious. He puffed himself up, straining the gold chain across his stomach.

"You take care of that wench of yours, Paul Swensson!" he roared. "First she stands there making eyes to a fool of a cobblemaker, who lives in a hut so small it could go inside my dog house. And the next minute she wants to marry a wafflebaker."

Yes, that's what he said. And now Pernilla understood that she had heard wrongly, and that Frans was not a wafflebaker, but a cobbler. And she had managed it so that she couldn't marry anybody but a wafflebaker. For what a person has sworn, a person must live up to.

Frans, standing beside them, heard what Jöns Oredsson said. He understood it all, too, for he was quick at grasping things, that's for sure. Poor Pernilla hid her face in her apron and cried, while her father pulled her after him. But Frans was happy, because now he knew it was him she wanted. He was going to find a way out. He walked over to the hardware store where he wanted to buy a knife he needed to carve his wooden shoes. While standing there, thinking and searching among the knives, he saw Madam Chrusander, the dean's wife, come in and buy a waffle iron. She said that the kitchen maid had let her beloved old, inherited iron fall on the stone floor and two of the hearts had been broken.

When Frans heard that he jumped up. He quickly counted his pennies and saw that they would just stretch to a waffle iron. And that was what he bought instead of a knife. Then he took the waffle iron under his arm, ran after the dean's wife, and told her everything. The dean's wife said that if anybody could teach him the art of baking waffles, it was she. For the finest waffle recipe in all Skane had gone down in her family for over a hundred years.

And then the dean's wife took Frans home with her to the parsonage. She brought him into the kitchen and put an apron on him. There he had to measure cream and flour and eggs and water, following her instructions. Then he whipped the batter and forced himself to wait until it rose. Everybody knows that waffle batter has to rise.

Finally it was time to begin the baking. The first waffle stuck to the iron.

"Everyone is a child to begin with," said the dean's wife and threw it in the pail for the pig.

The second one was pale and doughy.

"Better luck next time," said the dean's wife and gave it to the cat.

The third one he burned a little at the edges,

"That one was almost there," said the dean's wife and gave it to her pet pug dog.

The fourth one was just right. All five hearts were golden and crisp.

"Chrusander!" called the dean's wife, opening the study door a little. The dean came out and broke off a heart. His wife took another and they both said, Ah! when they ate it.

Frans swung his iron, and baked a huge pile of delicious waffles. And when the batter was used up, he thanked them for what he had learned, and then he wanted to take his iron and leave.

But the dean said, "Beata, dear, wouldn't it be better if he took the waffles to sell in the market, now that he has become a real wafflebaker?"

"You said it, Chrusander!" said his wife.

Well, I can tell you Frans was happy. He hurried off to the market with all his waffles in a basket. After him waddled the dean's wife, and after her trotted the dean. And the dean had made a big sign which said: "FOR SALE! NEWLY BAKED WAFFLES!" which he hung above the booth.

When Frans arranged his waffles on the counter beside the wooden shoes, a crowd gathered around his stand. Everybody bought and ate and praised his waffles. And suddenly Pernilla and her father were there, and behind them stood Jöns Oredsson. Jöns's red face became almost pale green, when he discovered the dean's sign. But Pernilla turned red as a rose, and smiled at Frans, and Frans smiled at Pernilla.

"Is this the wafflebaker you want?" asked Pernilla's father.

"Yes, dear father, this is the one," said Pernilla.

"This is lying and cheating," screamed Jöns Oredsson. "That fellow is a cobblemaker from the hut down by the cross road! Those waffles must have been stolen from the innkeeper's kitchen."

At that, Dean Chrusander stepped forward and stuck his chubby forefinger in Jöns Oredsson's stomach.

"That's a lie, Jöns Oredsson," he said. "My wife and I stood beside Frans as he baked those delicious waffles. So he truly is a wafflebaker, and to that we can attest."

"Chrusander is right, and Jöns Oredsson ought to be ashamed," said the dean's wife.

Jöns Oredsson became so enraged, he stuck his stomach out so far that his gold chain burst. With that he slunk on home.

But Frans broke off a piece of the last waffle and offered it to Pernilla.

"May I give you a heart? I have saved it for you alone," he said.

"Thank you very much," answered Pernilla with a curtsy and took his hand. And Frans didn't let go of her hand after that.

Pernilla's father said that since the dean himself had come to speak for Frans, he, Paul Swensson from South Ridge, was not the man to say no.

Well, after that, you know what happened, of course. Dean Chrusander married Frans and Pernilla, and the dean's wife gave them the waffle recipe for a wedding gift. And Frans lived happily ever after with his Pernilla, and baked waffles as long as he lived.

It's a long time since this happened. Only the cottage and the sign are left. They are both well worn, and will soon be on their last legs, I should say. But the climbing roses which Pernilla planted are just as nice as ever. Then, of course, she did bring those plants with her from South Ridge, where, so they say the girls and the roses are the prettiest in all Skane."

"Oh," cried grandmother from inside, and they heard her rattling the pans. "Here I stay and listen and burn the last rolls."

"That was too bad," said Mons the Thatcher, pouring himself another drop of coffee. "Well what did you think about this story?"

"It was fine," said Kaja emphatically.

"Yes, even if it was a girl story, though," said Pelle-Göran.

"But Frans was a man, wasn't he?" said Kaja. "And Jöns Oredsson, that mean one, and the dean and Pernilla's Pappa . . ."

"I know what he means," said Mons. "Of course, you're right. The girls are the ones who really like the stories about people who fall in love and marry."

"Don't you know some stories about boys, too?" asked Pelle-Göran, wiping the juice mustaches off his mouth with a sticky little paw.

"Oh, yes, some other time," said Mons the Thatcher.

Grandmother was muttering something inside.

"All that show and flattery, he was spreading it on a little too much," she said, cleaning the pan.

Mons leaned over to the children, and whispered: "You see, your grandmother, she belongs to the Roses from South Ridge, too, and they've always been a little modest about themselves. You ought to have seen how grand she looked when she was young. But now I must go and rip out the last part before Folke comes back with the new straw."

Grandmother came out to get the tray.

"In with you children and wash. It's time to go to town. And thank you for the entertainment, Mons."

"I am the one who should thank you for the refreshments," said Mons the Thatcher, bowing and swinging his slouchy hat in a wide circle. "Oh, but just look now," he said squinting towards the barn. "My small partners, they certainly are faithful."

There, on the roof strolled the cats. The last kitten was just climbing up the ladder.

"Well, I can't help laughing," said grandmother. "Just imagine how they've used the opportunity!"

"Is that why you didnt' take down the ladder when you went off?" asked Kaja.

"Well," said Mons the Thatcher, "you see, they had asked me to leave it."

"Oh-h," said Pelle-Göran.

But he wasn't quite sure about it all.

10

Grandmother's Walk to School

The road to the clogmaker's went through the forest. They hadn't walked very far before they saw a family of rabbits playing in the clearing. Kaja cried out in delight and —psst—they were gone.

"If only we could catch one of them and take him home with us," said Kaja.

"They aren't so easy to catch, those little long legs," said grandmother. "And they certainly are much better off where they are, than in captivity. But one summer when I was a child, I really had a tame little rabbit."

"Lucky you!" said Kaja.

"Father found him in the forest and brought him home to me. He became as tame as a cat and followed me wherever I went. Nobody else was allowed to feed him, and he ate in my lap. And always, before he touched his food, he got up on his hind legs, beating my dress with his forepaws. Mother said perhaps it was the rabbits' way of saying grace."

"What did he eat?"

"Turnips and carrots and cabbage leaves and all kinds of greens."

"Where did he go? Did he die later on?" asked Pelle-Göran.

"No, in the fall I sold my nice Jösse for one krona and fifty," said grandmother, sounding a bit ashamed.

"Oh, but how could you, grandmother!" said Kaja shocked.

"Yes indeed, how could I! It was a hard thing to decide to do. But you see, there was something I wanted so much to buy, and it cost one krona and fifty. One krona and fifty was a lot of money in those days. And the farmer who wanted to buy Jösse from me was known all over South Ridge for his kindness to animals. All sorts of deer would come to him and eat out of his hand. His baby pigs ran in and out of his house. So I thought that with him Jösse would at least have a good home."

"That's the kind of a man I am going to marry," said Kaja.

Pelle-Göran asked curiously what it was grandmother had wanted to buy with the money.

"A porcelain egg hen," said grandmother sighing a little.

"The one in the big room at home?"

"Yes, that's the one. It will be—let me see—yes, forty-eight years this fall."

"Well, it looks nice and grand. But I can't imagine why you wanted that one instead of a real little rabbit?" said Kaja disapprovingly.

"Well, you see, it was fashionable around here at that time to serve eggs in that kind of hen at Easter time. All the neighbors had them. And I was so childish that I felt ashamed we didn't have one. It was my vanity hen, that one. But I had no sooner carried it home to mother from the store in Kageröd, than I regretted it. After that I saved all my pocket money thinking that I might get together enough to buy my Jösse back again. But it never happened. One winter morning we discovered rabbit tracks outside the shed in which I had kept Jösse. I knew then he had run away and come back trying to get in. We left the door ajar in case he might try it again. But he never returned. And he never came back to Ore Farm where I had sold him. I suppose he ran into the forest to stay with the wild rabbits."

"Maybe those little rabbits we saw were Jösse's children?" said Pelle-Göran.

But grandmother and Kaja thought perhaps they might be Jösse's greatgreatgreatgreatgreatgreatgreat grandchildren or so.

"This is where I used to walk to school in the old days," said grandmother. I often used to see roe deer. And once I saw a family of elk over there. I can still remember how cute that little elk child was as it walked between its parents on tall thin legs. And once in a while it happened that a fox would streak across the road like a red bit of lightning.

"You were frightened, weren't you, grandmother?"

"Oh, foxes don't dare to attack people, and I knew that. But sometimes it did feel a little spooky walking here, especially early on dark winter mornings, or when I was going home after dark. Then I imagined I saw trolls and wolves everywhere."

"Oh, there aren't any trolls," said Pelle-Göran.

"But we did have wolves here earlier, although there aren't any left here now. And one time when I had sandwiches, with honey on in my lunch box, I was afraid that a bear would come and catch me. For I had heard that bears loved honey and could smell it from far off. I ran so fast my side hurt. And as I was running past one of those big boulders, I saw something big and black moving behind it. A bear! I thought, of course, although there hasn't been a bear on South Ridge since long before my time. But, it was only Henning Andersson's black and white cow. I was so relieved that I offered her a honey sandwich. And, just imagine, she didn't want it."

"You tell stories like a thatcher," said Kaja.

"More, more," begged Pelle-Göran putting his hand into grandmother's, he who never liked to hold anybody's hand.

But now they were out of the forest, and not far from the clogmaker. And he didn't live in any old cabin with climbing roses and a gilded sign, but in a very ordinary house of yellow brick with a porch and a flagpole. And he didn't really have such happy and lively eyes either. But, that he made fine wooden shoes, they could see from those on which he was working.

The clogmaker stood the children on a piece of paper on the floor. Then he traced their feet with a flat carpenter's pencil, made marks and crosses, measured with a yellow tape measure, examined their soles and wrote it all down in a book.

"They'll be ready next Thursday," he said.

And that was all.

Grandmother must have noticed that they seemed to feel a little let down when they were leaving.

"Well, you see, Erik Persson isn't quite as lively as that Frans," she said. "But after all, who really knows about Frans? Mons the Thatcher is a clever man, of course, but he adds to things, and decorates everything he talks about, so it all sounds wonderful. It's rather hard for him to keep his feet on the ground."

"Yes, he walks on the roof, of course," said Pelle-Göran.

11

Can Lubbe Talk?

"Sixteen, seventeen, eighteen . . ."

Pelle-Göran was sitting on the steps counting corks. He had heard that if he could save two hundred it would make a swimming pillow. And that was just what he needed as he could not swim. With a swimming pillow he could float like a cork himself and follow the little paper boats in their race down the brook.

He had been begging for the old corks from all the juice and medicine bottles which grandmother and Dela had. He had searched the attic and the basement. He even had picked up some corks from the garbage pile. But yet it wasn't enough. He still would have to save for a long time.

Kaja had counted them twice for him. The first time she got seventy-eight. The second time it came out eighty-two.

Well, what was it, really? It couldn't be seventy-eight and eighty-two both.

"Nineteen, tineteen, elvteen, twelteen, thirteen . . ."

Kaja was in the barn just then, helping Dela strain the evening milk. So he would have to try counting for himself. It didn't go very well. Whatever he did, it came out differently every time. And it never became seventy-eight or eighty-two, only twelteen, or fourteen or so . . .

"Grandmother, please help me count," he called in to the kitchen.

Grandmother said she had no time because she was getting the supper ready. And Folke, of course, was busy, too, for Mons the Thatcher was in there. They probably had something important to talk over. And Stig had gone home to Klövatorp on his bicycle.

"Fourteen, fifteen, sixteen, eighteen, nineteen, tineteen, elvteen. . . ."

Grandmother called to Lubbe, "Come here, Lubbe, I've got something for you."

She rarely gave the dog and the cat something to eat in the kitchen. Most of the time they had their food outside.

Lubbe came trotting across the yard, leaped right over Pelle-Göran and disappeared into the kitchen.

"Twelteen, thirteen, fourteen," counted Pelle-Göran loudly, pushing the corks he had counted aside.

Then he heard voices from the kitchen, grandmother's and that of a stranger. Did she have guests, although he hadn't seen anybody going in the house?

"Are you talking with somebody, grandmother?" he called curiously.

Grandmother didn't answer right away. There were sounds of mumbling and smothered laughter from the kitchen. And when she answered, it sounded as if she were still laughing a little.

"What did you say, who am I talking to? Oh, only to Lubbe."

He went on counting loudly. Then he suddenly stopped in surprise. That other voice, when it talked, it sounded as if it growled and yapped at the same time.

"A piece of meat!" it growled and yapped. "Please, Mother Klara, please give me a little bit of meat! I'm so hungry."

"No, look here! You eat that porridge, it was cooked this

morning," said grandmother. "And that bone, you can still gnaw on that for a long time."

"A bite of meat! Only one little bite!" yapped that strange voice.

"Oh well then, sit up nicely and I'll give you a sausage skin," said grandmother.

"A little more! I'm thirsty too," whined the voice.

"Here is water," said grandmother, and there was the splashing of water as she poured it out.

Pelle-Göran sat on the steps with open mouth. No, he thought, it couldn't be true. It couldn't be Lubbe talking.

"Can't I have a little milk," fretted the peevish voice.

"No, little Lubbe, you're too fat already," said grandmother.

"Lubbe!" she said.

Pelle-Göran jumped up and dashed into the kitchen so fast he stumbled and fell right across Lubbe and the dish of water. His clothes were soaked in the front but he didn't hurt himself. He couldn't make himself get up, he just lay there on the floor looking around. In the whole kitchen he saw only grandmother and Lubbe, nobody else! Carefully he looked around. The door to the pantry wasn't quite closed, of course. There was just a little opening. But guests didn't usually go in the pantry, though?

"I don't suppose you hurt yourself, since you're not crying?" said grandmother.

"Lubbe," said Pelle-Göran, struggling up. "Is it true? Can you talk, Lubbe?"

Busily licking up the spilled water, the dog stopped,

looked at him and opened his mouth, but not to talk, just to yawn, a huge uninterested yawn.

"Answer!" cried Pelle-Göran. "Say something, if you can, Lubbe."

Grandmother smiled.

"Lubbe is still a little shy in front of you. If you go out he might feel a little more free."

Reluctantly Pelle-Göran moved out toward the back entrance. But he left the door open for he would rather see than just hear Lubbe talk.

But everything was quiet. The only thing he heard was a slight creaking some place, almost like rusty hinges.

"I think you'll have to go farther away," said grandmother.

He went as far as to the outer door, although he couldn't see Lubbe from there. And then . . .

"Close that door after you, lad, and don't stand there spying," the dog growled angrily.

The dog! Could it really be the dog?

"Grandmother!" called Pelle-Göran. "Come and shake my hand and look me straight in the eyes and tell me that it is Lubbe speaking."

"Dumbbell!" growled the dog. "Who else could it be? Perhaps you think that Mother Klara sounds like this?"

But as the dog was saying all that, Pelle-Göran had cautiously sneaked over to the kitchen door. And he saw that Lubbe was busily gnawing on a big calf bone and grandmother was standing at the stove laughing, while she was emptying the potato water into a pail. None of them talked. But still that voice continued to yap, "Meat, please, Mother Klara, just a little piece of meat."

But wait! That little opening into the pantry! Wasn't it wider now? And wasn't that from where the voice came?

"Haha!" cried Pelle-Göran, rushing over there. The door closed with a bang. And he could not open it, no matter how much he tried. He turned the key and twisted at it. He pounded with his fists, calling out, "Open up!" But it didn't help one bit. The door was really locked, or else someone stood on the other side holding it.

"Grandmother," panted Pelle-Göran. "Come and help me. I can't get it open."

"What do you want in the pantry? Supper is almost ready," said grandmother, taking her time. She calmly put the potato kettle down and fixed the rings on the stove before she came over to try the lock.

"Hurry," cried Pelle-Göran impatiently.

"I think you have done something to the lock," she said, carefully wriggling and turning the key back and forth.

It took a little while. But finally she got the door open. The hinges creaked when Pelle-Göran anxiously pushed past her and in.

Empty! Not even a cat was in there. Nothing but the usual jars and cooky boxes, and bags and that blue Höganäs crock with spiced herring. And in the draught from the open window swung a bunch of dried gray marjoram, which grandmother had said was used to add taste to the pea soup.

"You must be terribly hungry since you are in such a hurry," said grandmother. "I suppose I'd better give you some gingerbread and butter to keep you going for a bit."

They stood quietly in the pantry while grandmother buttered a big piece of gingerbread.

Maybe it was Lubbe after all. Or could whoever growled and yapped have climbed out through the window, perhaps?

He looked out. No, nobody was there. If he already hadn't gone around the corner, of course.

"I think we'll close it so the flies won't come in on the food," said grandmother, and pulled the window in. "Well, aren't you going to have your gingerbread?"

"Yes, thank you. But grandmother, take my hand and look me in the eyes . . ."

What was that? A voice reached the two in the pantry. A yapping, growling voice.

"Meat, please, Mother Klara! Don't keep me waiting any longer! Come out and give me a little meat!"

It came from the kitchen. Then it was the dog. Pelle-Göran peeked through the door. Yes, only Lubbe was there.

But what was it he glimpsed outside through the open kitchen window in between the geraniums? A head and a pair of broad rugged shoulders!

Pelle-Göran shot across the floor and tore aside the blue checkered curtain. Outside stood Mons the Thatcher looking in. He looked red and perspiring and puffed a little as if he had been running.

"Haha, it was you, Mr. Thatcher," shrilled Pelle-Göran. "I knew it! I knew it!"

Mons the Thatcher looked innocent and puzzled.

"Yes, of course it's me," he said surprised. "Who did you think it might be? A cow perhaps? Or Reynard the fox? Well, Mother Klara, I only wanted to say good evening and thank you for today. And now, I'll be trotting off."

"I am sure it was you anyway!" sang Pelle-Göran, hopping around on one foot with his gingerbread in his hand. "Yaha, I'm sure about it."

But neither grandmother nor Mons the Thatcher bothered to listen to him.

"But first you must have a little supper, Mons," said grandmother. "We'll soon eat."

"Thank you, Mother Klara, but you mustn't go to extra trouble for my sake," said Mons the Thatcher.

Pelle-Göran listened. The thatcher talked in a deep bass voice. It didn't sound like that yapping voice, at all. And yet there was something which reminded him of it. Perhaps it was because he said Mother Klara and so did the voice. Pelle-Göran hadn't heard anybody else calling her that.

"Come in, anyway," said grandmother.

The head disappeared from the window, and soon after the thatcher came in. In the door he met Lubbe. The dog was in a hurry, for Amelie stood outside quacking disapprovingly. Her quacking sounded like, "Where in the world have you been? I have been so worried."

Pelle-Göran felt completely bewildered.

"Did you know, Mr. Thatcher, that Lubbe could speak Skanish?" he said.

"Yes, of course he does. It would be funny if he talked Upplandish. He is a Skaner, you know," said the thatcher sounding quite indignant.

"Oh no, Lubbe is a Newfoundlander," said grandmother, laughing in her sleeve.

"Oh, oh, I almost had forgotten that," said Mons the Thatcher.

"How does it sound that Newf- Newf . . . I mean, how does that language sound?" asked Pelle-Göran.

"Newfoundlandish? Let me see," said Mons. "Well, I don't know too much about it. I only know a little song which the people from Newfoundland like to sing sometimes in the evenings when they sit around cleaning their rifles. This is the way it goes." And then he sang:

"Yes box all right Virginia
And sinkabirikum.
Come on valeriana
Mixtum compositium.

A Yankee Doddle Dandy
Goodby Kentucky home
Krambambu balalaika
And magnum bonicomb."

Grandmother laughed. But she probably didn't want to hurt the feelings of Mons, since she turned away and kept the corner of her apron up to her face when she laughed.

"What does the song mean?" asked Pelle-Göran.

"It is our 'A Maiden went to the well for water,' in Newfoundlandish," said Mons. "I should have thought you would have known that from the melody. It's a pretty song and there are many more verses, but I have forgotten the others."

"Sing it once more," begged Pelle-Göran.

But now Dela and Kaja came in and grandmother sent Pelle-Göran after Folke who was taking a rest. And then it was time to eat supper.

Just as they were sitting down to the table, Pelle-Göran discovered something which made him open his eyes and mouth.

"Haha, haha!" he screamed. "Now I know. Now I really know."

"What is it you know?" wondered Folke.

"Haha! Yes, that dogs can't talk!"

"How do you know that?" said Kaja.

"Haha, hurrah, for Mr. Thatcher has got marjoram in his hair!" shouted Pelle-Göran joyously. "He was the one who stood in the pantry talking Lubbe language, haha, hurrah!"

Mons the Thatcher looked a little sheepish as he picked off the little gray branch that had stuck behind his ear.

"You sure have your eyes with you, lad," he said.

"Not that I understand a word of what you are talking about, but food is good anyway," said Folke grabbing three slices of cold lamb roll on his fork.

"You must have had fun while we were gone," said Kaja. "Can't we hear some Lubbe language, too?"

Mons the Thatcher laughed.

"Sure, if I can amuse the little lady with such a small thing."

"Meat," he yapped. "Can't the rest of us get a little piece of meat before Folke eats it all, that and the china, too."

They all laughed, Folke best of all. And grandmother saved the meat dish from her hungry son and offered it to Mons.

"It was too bad, though, that it wasn't Lubbe talking," said Pelle-Göran thoughtfully.

"You think so?" said Mons the Thatcher. "Well, don't be too sure. Next time maybe it will be Lubbe talking."

"Silly!" said Pelle-Göran.

12

The Snake Bite

One morning Stig's sister was standing by the gate again. She had come all the long way from Klövatorp to Stubba Farm with a huge eel for grandmother. It was in a bag which she carried on her back.

"We caught it ourselves in our brook, and mother says to give it to Mrs. Bengtsson and say thanks for all kindnesses," she rattled off in a shrill voice.

Grandmother wanted to pay for it, but that wouldn't do at all. She was to have it as a "gift," said Ellen, frowning as if grandmother had said something very wrong. So grandmother quickly thanked her and accepted it. Folke smacked his lips and said that oven baked eel was about the best food he knew. And then grandmother asked if Ellen wouldn't like to stay and play with the children and sleep there overnight.

Ellen gave Pelle-Göran and Kaja a quick glance. Then she said she would see, but that mother had said she might sleep in the harness room if Mrs. Bengtsson would let her. Grandmother said that would be fine. But then Kaja asked if all of them might sleep in the barn instead. And grandmother said they could do that, of course, if they thought it such fun.

"We could lie there and tell stories," whispered Pelle-Göran.

"Ghost stories," said Kaja. "You aren't afraid of ghost stories, are you, Ellen?"

"Not if Stig is with me," said Ellen.

"Of course he is going to be with us," said Kaja and took her arm. "Come and see our kittens, Ellen!"

Ellen looked at all the kittens and said confidently that Tigerpaw was going to be the best hunter, and that its floppy ear didn't matter a bit, she was sure. So Pelle-Göran was happy. They took the kittens with them to the hayloft and played with them in the hay. Later on they went for a swim in the brook, and then Kaja suggested that they should go and see if there were any ripe blackberries yet. They followed the old stone fence and picked the blackberries which were ripe, but most of them were still green.

When they passed the little cottage, they saw Ola Gädda standing outside digging.

"Look, there is your grandfather," said Kaja.

"I don't care about 'm," mumbled Ellen.

Pelle-Göran called out: "Hi there! Here we come with Ellen from Klövatorp!"

The old man looked up quickly.

"Oh yes, yes, good day to you young'uns," he said.

But Ellen didn't look at him. She went past with her nose in the air, searching for blackberries as if she hadn't heard. Kaja jabbed her in the side.

"Aren't you going to say hello to your grandfather?"

"I can't stand mean old men," said Ellen in a loud clear voice.

"Sh-h!" whispered Kaja, shocked. "He can hear you!"

Ellen tossed her head. One could see she meant, "What of it, I don't care." And then she walked on.

Pelle-Göran saw that Ola Gädda looked thoughtfully after the girl. He climbed up on the gate.

"I'll tell you what," he whispered eagerly. "She is nice, though, even if William Nilsson and the others are mean to her and call her pilfer-lassie. She gave grandmother a fish that long and that big."

Ola Gädda wrinkled his bushy eyebrows.

"So, they're calling that little one a pilferer," he mumbled.

"Yes, even though it only was her Pappa who once stole an old fishing thing," said Pelle-Göran.

Then he ran after the girls.

"I like your grandfather," he said.

"You can go on doing that," said Ellen. "You can have him. I don't want him."

"Thank you, then I'll take Ola Gädda for a grandfather," said Pelle-Göran delightedly.

"My, how silly you are," said Ellen and jumped up on the stone fence, running along it on her bare feet. She had

left her wooden shoes in the entrance to the kitchen.

The blackberry runners were thorny, but she was hopping cleverly from one stone to another without touching the runners. Kaja and Pelle-Göran were left far behind.

Suddenly they heard her scream. It was not a very nice word she used, and they could tell she was frightened.

"What is it? Did you hurt yourself?" called Kaja.

"A snake," cried Ellen. "I stepped on him! He bit me in the foot. Oh-o-oh, I'll die-e-e!"

"Oh, that's terrible," cried Kaja close to tears. "What are we going to do? Where is it? Wait, I'll get a stick and kill it."

"He's gone," groaned Ellen. "He slid in among the stones."

She came limping towards them, the tears streaming down her cheeks. She didn't look so fierce any more.

"Oh, I can't walk. It's stinging like a knife."

"I am going to get Ola Gädda," said Pelle-Göran.

And off he ran as fast as he could.

The old man stood there, leaning on his spade, staring at something far off. It looked as if he hadn't stirred an inch since they had left him.

"Oh please," puffed Pelle-Göran. "Come right away. A snake has bitten Ellen's foot. She is dying!"

The old man turned slowly to him.

"What was it ye said?"

"I said that Ellen from Klövatorp stepped on a snake with her bare foot, so she is dying," said Pelle-Göran impatiently.

Then the old man came alive. He didn't walk through the gate. He shot over the fence like a crazy cow. And he ran along the path so fast Pelle-Göran could hardly keep up with him.

They heard Ellen moaning and Kaja sobbing. The girls were sitting in the middle of the path. Kaja had thrown one arm around Ellen, the other she was waving wildly around as if against imaginary snakes.

When Ola Gädda reached them he said, "Where is the bite? Show me the marks so I can suck out the poison."

Ellen stretched her foot out, crying and pointing. Kaja stopped waving her arm around. Pelle-Göran stood near the old man, in case there might be more vipers. Ola Gädda set his toothless mouth to the swollen foot and began sucking and spitting it out, sucking and spitting. Then he rose and lifted Ellen.

"Run, young'uns," he said to Kaja and Pelle-Göran. "Run and tell Folke Bengtsson to get the car ready, so we can go to the hospital. I'm coming with her as fast as I can."

They rushed home. But Folke had gone to Astorp for phosphate. Grandmother called the doctor. He promised to come at once and bring the snake serum.

When Ola Gädda came with Ellen she had stopped moaning. But she was still and pale, and her eyes were big and frightened.

"So, so, little one, it be not dangerous," said Ola Gädda in his rough voice and sat down beside her on the oak chair. He stroked her hair awkwardly. "So, so, it'll sure be better when the doctor gets here."

Pelle-Göran ran over to the east field for Stig.

"It isn't so dangerous, Stig," he said. "Grandmother says that one hardly ever dies from snake bite."

Stig didn't say a word, but how he ran! Pelle-Göran was so worn out from all his running that he was left far behind. When he reached home, Ellen had been carried into grandmother's bed. And grandmother and Ola Gädda and Stig were with her, while Kaja lifted out the cage with Julius, who fluttered around and screamed at the top of his voice, "Oh, how nice it is at Stubba Farm."

"Grandfather sucked out the poison, Stig," whispered Ellen.

Stig pressed her hand and nodded a little to Ola Gädda

who was sitting at the edge of a chair, squeezing his cap. But the old man didn't notice it. He saw nobody but the girl.

When the doctor arrived, everybody but grandmother had to leave. They sat in the kitchen, waiting. The parrot cage was standing on the sink. Again and again Julius proudly called out the new sentence which Kaja had taught him, "Oh, how nice it is at Stubba Farm!" Finally Dela spread a towel over the cage to silence him. For nobody thought it was so nice at Stubba Farm just now, since this had happened to poor Ellen.

They heard the doctor go out to the car and drive off. Then grandmother came and said that the doctor didn't think there was any danger, for the bite had not hit any vein. But to be on the safe side he had given the girl both serum and cortisone, and now, all she would have to do, was to stay quiet and everything would be all right. The doctor was going to look in on her later in the evening, because he would be coming this way then.

When Ola Gädda heard that he cheered up. Then he went to the door and peeked into grandmother's room.

"The lassie is a-sleeping now," he said softly. "She is a dear, isn't she?"

"Yes, she is," said grandmother. "Although she is a little cross and stubborn once in a while, of course."

"I've heard them say I'm that, too," said Ola Gädda. "But I've no use for folks who go around smiling all the time."

"Yes, well can we see that you two are kinfolks," said grandmother.

Then Ola Gädda smiled. It was the first time the children had seen him do that.

"Keep in mind that I aim to pay the doctor," he said.

"Yes, that isn't too much to ask," said grandmother. "And it is said that you have plenty of money put away, although you've let your daughter-in-law and her children fare so badly."

"Rubbish," said Ola Gädda annoyed. "For a long time I've been thinkin' about going home to Klövatorp after we get in the rye."

"Well, finally a sensible word," said grandmother happily.

"Ya, maybe they can use a man around the farm," said Ola Gädda, sullenly.

"You can be sure of that," said grandmother.

"And now we won't talk any more about that old affair."

"Well, if you can let bygones be bygones, I certainly can," said grandmother. "But if you hadn't dug up all that old stuff and moved away from Klövatorp, it would have been hidden and forgotten long ago, and nobody here at the Ridge would have given it a second thought."

Ola Gädda left, but in the evening when the doctor's car swung up in front of the house he came back again. He talked alone with the doctor. After the doctor had left grandmother asked the old man to stay for supper. He didn't say much at the table, but he looked happier than he had for a long time.

As they sat there they suddenly heard Ellen calling,

"Pelle-Göran!" And when he ran in she was lying in grandmother's bed looking at an album of photographs. She had borrowed Kaja's dotted pajamas and grandmother had combed her hair with water. Perhaps that was why she looked so unusually good and sweet.

"You go to the cottage and get him for me," she said.

"Who?"

"Grandfather," said Ellen.

"He is sitting in the kitchen," said Pelle-Göran.

"I want him in here," said Ellen.

"You didn't want him for a grandfather any longer. You gave him to me."

"I'm taking him back," said Ellen.

And Ola Gädda got up at once and went in to the patient.

"Well," said Kaja, "I suppose we can't stay in the barn tonight, now when Ellen can't go with us. What a pity! And we were going to tell ghost stories." "You can sleep in the barn some other time," said grandmother. "And telling stories you can do just as well up in your gable room."

"But what about Ellen?"

"Ellen ought to sleep," said grandmother.

"Oh no, I'm not sleeping," they heard from grandmother's room. "I've slept all day, so I'm awake now. It doesn't hurt any more either. Sure, I can stay in the hay. You promised to tell me stories."

"Listen to her," said Folke. "She isn't dying this year, that one."

"You'll have to stay where you are," said grandmother

when she had looked in on Ellen. "But if you feel that well, I suppose you may have a little story, although it better not be a ghost story."

They all gathered around the bed. Ola Gädda sat far over in a corner.

"Now, who is going to tell?" said grandmother. "Kaja, perhaps?"

But Kaja said she couldn't think of anything but two ghost stories, and Pelle-Göran didn't know any stories at all. Stig was too shy. They didn't even think about asking Ola Gädda.

"Folke, then?" asked grandmother.

Folke peered teasingly at Kaja and then he began.

"Once upon a time there was a girl as thin as a rail. She came from the north and traveled south. She had black hair and a white nose and gray eyes and a green mouth, I almost said. No, I suppose the mouth must have been red. And under her chin she had a light red rose almost as big as the whole girl. Yes, Ellen, you never saw such a rose in all your life. But then it came from the North Pole, and I suppose they grow like that up there."

"Shame on you, Folke, you are teasing!" said Kaja. "I am not any rail. But you are fat as a sausage, is that any better?"

"Well, there you have it, Folke?" said grandmother.

"Sausage," said Folke. "Sausage is good food. When I get hungry again after that wonderful meal of eel, I am going to get myself some sausage sandwiches. But I haven't said it was you. There are other pretty girls I would think."

"Please, go on," said Pelle-Göran.

141

"Well, that girl I am thinking of liked animals a lot, both dogs and cats, rhinos and gorillas and cuckoos and poisonous snakes and mosquitoes and wasps and snails and . . ."

"No-ho," said Kaja, "I don't either."

"But she didn't like people as well as she liked animals," continued Folke. "Especially people who were fat as sausages and had guns hanging on the wall."

"No, you are right there, of course," said Kaja.

"But one of those people who had guns on the walls and was fat as a sausage, he liked that little rail of a girl, even though he almost fell backwards when he saw that big red rose."

"Such a silly story," said Kaja annoyed. "And you let my rose alone."

"Now, Folke," said grandmother. "You know she got it from her best friend."

But Folke continued without paying heed. "Well, as mentioned before, he liked her very much. And the angrier she became at him, the more he liked her, for he liked girls who showed a little spunk. And he thought that seven years would be long enough in which to eat as much as he wanted, so after that he would not like food that well. Then he would stop eating and become as thin as a rail. And then he might tell her the truth that never had he fired a shot with those guns hanging on his wall since his father's time. For his father had been a real hunter, and his father's father and his mother's father and three of his brothers, too. But not he."

"Oh-oh," burst out Kaja. "You don't mean . . ."

142

"Only that this fatso was exactly as great an animal friend as that rail of a girl. No, I am not telling the truth. He made an exception to horseflies and mosquitoes and all kinds of bugs damaging the crop, that I must admit."

"Is that true, grandmother?" cried Kaja.

"Folke likes to argue, but he does not lie," said grandmother.

"There you see," said Folke. "And later on he was going to marry that rail of a girl and then they were going to live happily as long as they lived.

"On Stubba Farm?" asked Ellen who had listened breathlessly. "Oh, Folke Bengtsson, can't you take me instead?"

"Oh shush, girl!" said Stig blushing.

And Ola Gädda wriggled uneasily on his chair. But Folke said: "I'll think it over. We'll have to see in seven years. For the cuckoo told me I would not marry for seven years."

Ellen counted on her fingers to see how old she would be at that time.

"I guess it'll have to be Kaja then," she sighed.

"This is enough of nonsense," said Kaja. "In seven years I'll marry a jungle doctor, so you can have Folke. And now I think grandmother should tell a real story, for this one didn't count."

Grandmother said, "Oh sure, and what should that be about?"

"Ellen can decide, for she has the snake bite," said Pelle-Göran.

"Well, Ellen, what do you want to hear?"

"About snakes," said Ellen at once.

143

"Haven't you had enough of snakes, today?" asked grandmother.

"No-o," said Ellen.

"When I was little my mother used to tell about the snake king's daughter," said Folke.

"Oh, that one," said grandmother thoughtfully. "Yes, I think I still remember it."

"Hurry up and begin, grandmother," cried Pelle-Göran, crouching on the rug with his chin on grandmother's knee and his eyes wide open.

"I must have something in my hands if I am going to tell a story, give me my knitting, Kaja," said grandmother. "Well, this happened a long time ago. All of a hundred years ago. As for the story I am not sure that it happened at all, it may be that it is just an old tale."

"That won't matter, just tell it," said Ellen.

13

The Snake King's Daughter

And grandmother began:

"Once there was a farm in Stenestad, called the Brook Farm. It was left deserted because at that time there was a famine in Skane, and the owner had taken his wife and children with him over to Denmark. Soon the fields grew over, the buildings fell apart, bats and spiders settled in the house and beneath it swarmed rats and mice.

There were lots of snakes in the forest around here then, and around Snuve Halls especially, there were many."

"Usch!" said Kaja.

"The true animal friend loves even the poor snakes," recited Folke, rolling his eyes.

"Yes, it did happen that people were bitten while picking berries. Old people said that the snake king himself stayed in the big gravel pit there."

"I'm sure he was the one who bit me," said Ellen.

"But after the field mice and the rats had moved to the deserted farm, the snakes soon found their way there, too. For snakes live on such creatures."

"They eat leapers, too," said Ellen. "Mother said she saw a snake who ate a leaper alive."

Kaja and Pelle-Göran asked what a leaper was. Folke said it was a cross between an eagle and an elephant, but grandmother said it was a frog.

"And the years passed and soon the snakes had taken over the whole leaky old house. Nobody dared to go near it, and if any one had an errand in the vicinity, they walked way around the Brook Farm.

"But one day after many, many years a horse and buggy

drove into the yard. In the buggy sat an old woman and her son. As they had passed through the town of Stenestad some oldsters had recognized the woman as the one who once had been the mistress on Brook Farm. In her later years she had become so homesick she just couldn't stand it. Her husband had died and the older children had married in the Danish country. But the youngest son, Johannes, had come with her across the sound back to the old home.

"Well, the house was in such a bad condition that the nettles grew between the moldy floor boards and it rained in through the roof, besides all the damage the rats had done."

"Oh my, then it is much better at our place," said Ellen. "It's nice there, I'll tell you."

"Yes, Klövatorp is a very nice place," said grandmother.

Ola Gädda didn't say anything, but you could see he was pleased by this.

"But Johannes was a keen worker," said grandmother, "and he toiled from morning till night to get the farm in shape again. He chopped down trees for a new floor in the house, he built a new stove and he repaired the walls and the roof."

"Was it a thatched roof?" asked Pelle-Göran.

"I am sure it must have been. The bats under the eaves fluttered wide-awake out into the daylight. And when he began to tear up the rotten floor, there was a whole nest of snakes. "Sh-sh," they hissed, sliding out through the open door.

The mother let out a scream, "Did you see that huge

snake with the crown on his head, Johannes? It was the snake king himself!"

But Johannes thought the mother was only imagining things, and that the snake king was just an old superstition.

"That's what it is, isn't it?" asked Pelle-Göran.

"Remember that this is a tale," said grandmother. "Johannes said: "Well, then it was a good thing we got rid of him." Then he took up the crowbar again and broke loose the rotten boards. But the mother said, "Now we shall have to watch out. They will take revenge because we chased them out." But Johannes said the snakes were the intruders, and not he and his mother. Suddenly he noticed something glittering on the floor. When he picked it up he saw it was a little ring of the whitest silver, just big enough to fit his little finger. On one side it was smooth and round, but along the other side ran a border of fine, small scallops.

"Johannes, my dear son, throw that after the snakes," begged the mother. "It isn't a ring, at all, it is a crown. It must belong to some of the snake king's children. If we keep it, the snake people will never leave us in peace."

But Johannes didn't pay any attention to what she was saying. He thought it might just as well be a ring as a crown, and its seemed like a sign to him that he should have found a ring. Because on Spring Farm lived a girl named Boel, and he had been thinking about her ever since he first met her at church. Pretty and good and quick at work she was, and he had seen she didn't think badly of him either. He would like very much to have her for his wife when he got the farm in order again. Now he thought, he might propose to her and give her that ring so nobody else could run off with her.

And when he had finished his work that day, he walked over to Spring Farm and proposed. The girl and her parents were both happy and satisfied, for Johannes had already won a good name in the neighborhood for his diligence. So Boel took the ring, and promised to become his wife."

"Oh, it is going to be one of those girl stories again," muttered Pelle-Göran.

"Well, if you don't want to listen to it, you don't have to," said grandmother. "You can go to bed, if you like."

But Pelle-Göran didn't want to do that at all. So grandmother continued: "Boel looked at the ring and said, "It is

149

so lovely. It is almost like a little princess crown. But you didn't have to give me a ring, dear Johannes. I would have been faithful to you anyway."

Then she put the ring on her finger. It felt icy cold. But she thought it would soon get warm if she just wore it a little while. But it never did get any warmer, and it spread such a strange chilliness around it that her hands began feeling cold, just the way they felt when she used to clean frozen herring in the middle of winter. She had a feeling, too, that the cold was spreading right up her arm and straight towards her heart.

"It's just my imagination," she thought. And she talked happy and loving words to Johannes. So when he went home through the forest he was so happy he didn't know what were the tops and what were the roots of the trees.

But when he reached the farm, he saw a girl sitting on the steps, crying silently. She waved her head back and forth, and the tears glistened like diamonds in the moonlight. Johannes asked her who she was and why she was crying. She whispered that her name was Sisela and that she cried because she had lost her home and the dearest thing she owned. And now she didn't know what to do.

He thought she meant that she had lost her father and her mother. So he said that if she was a good worker, she might stay with him and his old mother for the time being. The girl rose and curtsied again and again, thanking him humbly. And then she whispered that she would do her best.

"Speak up so I can hear your voice," said Johannes. "He who whispers, lies."

But the girl waved her head like a flower on its stem when the wind is shaking it. And she whispered that she was born without a voice.

"Poor thing, then you can't sing when you work like my Boel does," said Johannes.

He looked at her and thought she was beautiful in a strange, foreign way, and he thought he had never before seen anybody move in such a soft and graceful way so that all the pretty girls at Stenestad would look big and clumsy beside her. Then he brought her in to his mother. The mother was very happy to have a servant in the house, so the girl stayed on and lived with them. She slept in the chimney corner and in the morning she was up long before the others. She did her chores quickly and silently. They hardly needed to ask her to do them before they were done. Even so the mother couldn't quite learn to like her.

"She is hissing like a snake instead of speaking like a human being," she said to her son. "She has asked to eat by herself in the chimney nook, but I never see her touch the food. She slides and glides in and out of corners and nooks, as if she were looking for something to steal."

But Johannes didn't want to listen. He hammered and he nailed, he put new glass in the empty windows and he fixed the new stove. And while he was working his eyes often went to Sisela, following her as she did her work. And there was less and less time to walk over to Spring Farm, and when he did he soon came back again.

One night he dreamed that Sisela came to him crying and asked for the ring he had given Boel. He became angry with her. So when he saw her the next morning he thought her eyes looked like snake eyes, and he talked harshly to her. But when she slid away crying, he felt sorry for her. The thoughts about Sisela disturbed him in his work. He became listless and often dropped what he was doing without finishing it.

But on Spring Farm Boel lay very ill. Her mother sat by her bedside day and night. The girl was so cold that neither hot stones nor warm jars in her bed could make her teeth stop chattering. When Johannes came visiting she didn't recognize him. And when he said, "It's me, Johannes," she answered, "Then you have changed a lot. And if you have changed your mind as well, take back your ring." But Johannes answered, "I'll abide by my word. When you get well, your mother shall have to prepare for a wedding." And then he left.

Boel cried for his voice had sounded so cold and strange. And when the mother left the bedroom to heat the stones at the fire again, she rose trembling and dressed. Then she sneaked out and dragged herself dizzy and tottering along to Brook Farm. It was far to walk, and although it was a warm summer evening, she shivered as in the middle of the winter.

Johannes hadn't gone straight home, but was wandering around in the forest. So he was not yet home when Boel arrived. But on the steps sat Sisela crying. Boel asked her who she was and why she was crying. But the girl didn't answer.

Boel said, "Move over so I can go in and speak to Johannes."

Then the girl whispered: "He isn't home yet. He has gone to see his betrothed." And she began crying again.

"If it is because of me you are crying," said Boel, "you can dry your tears. And if it is because of you my betrothed has become indifferent to me, you are the one he should have and not me."

Just then Johannes came out of the forest. When he saw Boel he was alarmed.

"Do you want to catch your death coming this long way, sick as you are," he said.

"It may well cost me my life," said Boel, "but I had to come and set you free. And here, you may have your ring back again."

"You are raving," said Johannes. "You are ill and you must get to bed right now."

But Boel pulled the ring off her finger and held it out to him. The ring glittered in the moonlight but Johannes didn't want to take it. But when Sisela saw it shining, she jumped up.

"My crown!" she whispered, and it sounded like a hissing. She threw herself over Boel and tore the ring out of her hand.

At that same moment Sisela vanished. But a slender and neat little snake with a silver crown on its head wound its way across the grass towards Snuve Halls.

And while Johannes and Boel stood there, staring in amazement after the snake, the warmth began coming back into Boel's cold body and her heart turned as warm as a beechwood fire.

"A snake!" said Johannes shuddering.

"The snake king's daughter," said Boel. "And just imagine, Johannes, I suddenly feel well again."

"I am also cured," said Johannes. "Can you forgive me?"

"Yes," she said, smiling, and then he took Boel's hand, smiling back at her with his own good smile.

"Come, let's go in to mother," he said.

14

Hoss Peter and the Konga Bull

Grandmother stopped talking.

"And then I suppose they lived happily until they died and were buried in Stenestad churchyard," said Folke. "Weren't they, mother?"

"It might not be impossible," said grandmother. "Although this is a story, of course, one does not know how much truth there may be to it. And just by taking a look at the old grave stones, one can see that many a Boel and many a Johannes lie buried there. So, who knows. But now it looks as if Ellen wants to sleep."

"I'm not sleeping, I'm just closing my eyes," said Ellen. "I'm thinking about that Sisela. I, too, would like to have such a silver crown."

Ola Gädda took out his worn wallet and held out a shiny one-krona coin to Ellen.

"This one is silver, too. And a krona is a crown," he said.

"Mother has told us we must not take money from strangers," said Ellen.

"Ye're grandfather isn't a stranger," said Ola Gädda.

Then she took the coin and lay there playing with it.

"Grandmother," said Pelle-Göran. "I do think, though, it is a shame I never get to hear a real boy story."

"That will come some other day," said grandmother.

" 'Another day,' Mons the Thatcher also said, but he didn't come to tell any more," mumbled Pelle-Göran.

Ola Gädda said quietly that he knew a story about Hoss Peter, and if nobody else knew it, he would try to tell it. Of course, those young ones from Uppland might not understand what he said because he, of course, spoke the way they used to talk in South Asby county in the olden times.

Grandmother said that if there was anything Pelle-Göran and Kaja couldn't understand, she could explain it to them. And she said that as a child she had heard about Hoss Peter, but most of the story she had forgotten now, and it would be very nice to hear it again.

And Ola Gädda began telling. The story was about a boy called Peter. He was very small, hardly any taller than Pelle-Göran even though he was thirteen years old. He came as farm hand to Grönhult, and there he learned to care for horses. One day the baron of Dragesholm happened to notice Peter riding the horses out to grass. He went to the Grönhult farmer and said: "This one is going to be a real horseman, and I would like to have him at Dragesholm." And that's how he came to go there. The other stable boys there laughed at him because he was so short, and a little bow-legged he was too.

They soon saw that he was unusually clever with horses, grooming them and riding in the young ones. So people began calling him Hoss Peter, for at that time there were many who called the horses "hosses." Some still do today as grandmother and Folke agreed.

The baron took such a liking to Peter that nobody but the boy was allowed to care for the new riding horse the baron had bought from England. The horse was young and rather wild. The baron himself could hardly check him, and he kicked and bit the other stable boys if they got in his way. But he was like a lamb with Peter. It could not be helped, however, that the boys became a little jealous of Peter because of the baron's and the horse's liking for him, and they tried to make trouble for him whenever they could. But he didn't pay much attention to them, he kept to the horses.

Now it so happened that at the time there was a lot of elk on South Ridge, much more than now. Among them was a huge savage elk bull walking around and making the region unsafe. One moment it was here, the next moment it was there. It had become the terror of all South Ridge for it had attacked and half-killed both people and cattle. It had no respect for stone fences and hedges and closed gates. It did damage to fields and gardens and young trees, and even though many had hunted it, all had failed, for when they sighted that huge crown and that giant humped up neck, they began to tremble and could not shoot straight. And there was much talk about a great hunter from Konga island who had been chased up into an oak tree and had to sit there a whole day while the elk bull was watching under the tree. Since that time the elk was called the Konga bull.

That Konga bull had done damage to Dragesholm, too. One day the baron came to the stable and talked to the boys about it. He said that if anybody could do away with the Konga bull, he could count on a real reward. Then one of the boys remarked that Hoss Peter, who was such a big and clever fellow, might catch that Konga bull. And the other one said that Hoss Peter who had such a good hand with animals, might even tame that beast. "Well, just wait, one fine day we might even see Hoss Peter come riding in on the Konga bull," he said scornfully.

But the baron said sternly that Hoss Peter had more sense than he had body, and that he was worth more than the two of them put together. So they had better leave him alone.

The boys, of course, didn't like that. And when Peter, a little later, came down to the pond to water the horses, they tripped him and he fell in. Well, he picked himself up again, there wasn't exactly any danger. But in the evening the boys chased him out of the servant's cottage where he had stayed with them, saying that for such a fine gentleman the cottage was altogether too plain and humble, and it would be better for him to seek finer lodgings.

Then Peter thought he might go out and spend the night in the pasture where the horses slept. Now, it so happened that the baron had quite a large orchard, and in one end of it there was something which he treasured above all. It was a

whole grove of Chinese lemon-
apple trees, around which he
had built a fence twice as big
and twice as strong as other
fences. Now when Hoss Peter
was going to the pasture he
walked through the orchard.
It was late spring and the buds
were just bursting.

As he came along he suddenly saw a terribly big animal
stretching its head over the tall fence trying to snatch a
branch from the Chinese trees. And when he stole closer he
knew that this must be the elk bull from Konga island, for
there could be no other animal as big as this one on the
whole Ridge.

He stood there hidden for a long time, watching the elk stretch and stretch and still not be able to reach any branch. He saw how it took a run at the fence, trying to leap over it. The fence, however, was too high, so then the elk began butting it to tear it down. But it was so strong it withstood all attempts. Finally the antlers became entangled in the fence and the bull couldn't get them loose.

Hoss Peter climbed over the fence. He broke off a few small twigs from the precious trees and walked towards the elk. Ever so carefully he wriggled loose the antlers. In a furious mood, the elk tried to attack him through the fence, but succeeded only in getting caught again. Hoss Peter began talking kindly and calmly, almost fatherly to the elk. Then once more he worked loose the antlers, and before it had time to attack him again, he stuck a twig under its muzzle. The elk snorted, but somehow, it happened, it took the twig and began chewing. Peter fed the elk twig after twig, talking to it all the time as he used to talk to the horses. Finally he ventured to stroke its muzzle. The elk was jerky and suspicious, but by and by it calmed down and in the end it gently sniffed at Peter's empty hand.

"Well, nothing more will be served today," said Peter.

And believe it or not, the elk left, quietly and good-naturedly. Peter climbed back over the fence and walked to the pasture and slept there all night.

The next morning when he led out the horse for the baron's ride the boys had made it their business to be around for they wanted to hear whether Peter would tell the baron that they had thrown him out. But Peter only said, "Say, baron, what would you give me if I rode up in front of the steps to Dragesholm on the Konga bull?"

The baron shouted with laughter, and even the boys laughed, although a little more cautiously.

"My dear Hoss Peter, the day you can do that, you may wish for anything I own and have," he said.

"Then I shall ask for the Chinese lemon-apple trees," said Peter.

"You aren't bashful, are you," said the baron, laughing even more. "The Chinese lemon-apple trees, which are the very rarest thing we have to show off here at Dragesholm! Even so, I feel sure, I can promise them to you. Yes, that and more, too. I think I safely can promise you the whole estate, for the Konga bull will never allow you or anybody else on its back."

"The trees will do," said Hoss Peter. "Now you have promised them to me, and Paul and Anders here are witnesses to that."

Late next evening he went back to the enclosure, and it wasn't very long before the elk bull appeared again. The same thing happened. The elk ate the twigs and Peter stroked its muzzle and chatted to it. Once in a while it would get impatient and try to butt, if it didn't have a twig the moment the other was eaten. But that was only in the beginning. Soon Peter could sit high on top of the fence with his arm around the elk's neck, while it ate out of his hand.

The summer passed and the elk came every night, becoming more and more tame. But if Peter tried to give it a twig from any tree but the lemon-apple trees, it shook its head in displeasure.

Then, one night late in August, Peter let one leg slide over the back of the elk, and suddenly he was sitting across it.

The elk flung up its head and snorting and lurching it galloped off into the forest. But Peter held on to the big shovel-like horns, all the time speaking soothingly to it in his usual fashion. Over hedges and stone fences went the bareback rider, and not before Magleröd did the elk begin to calm down a little. Still, they went zigzagging in through the forest, and out on the road, but when they came to Sjöbo Hills the Konga elk began to trot like a horse. And when they arrived at Munkabo, the elk and its rider were in complete accord. Then Peter leisurely rode back to Dragesholm. By the lemon-apple grove he stepped down, and by that time the elk was so worn out that it lay down on the ground and went to sleep.

But Peter broke off a whole armful of twigs from the Chinese lemon-apple trees, and stuck them down into the ground at certain intervals. Then he went back for more twigs. Finally he had planted a path of twigs all the way to the baron's bedroom window. When he was finished he went over and laid down beside the elk, and both of them slept until the sun rose. Then the elk woke up, stretched its legs and with its muzzle began pushing Peter for something to eat.

Peter awakened, got up and led the elk to the first twig he had planted. And while the elk was eating the first twig he took hold of the horns and swung himself up on its back. Then he steered the elk from twig to twig and the elk ate them all from the first one to the last one, which was standing just below the baron's window. There Peter took a little green apple from the twig, threw it at the window and called out, "Here I am with the Konga bull, baron!"

The baron woke up. Sleepily he opened the window and

stuck out his head with the nightcap on. When he saw the boy on the back of the bull, he rubbed his eyes, and thought he must be dreaming. But again Peter called, "Yes, here I am with the Konga bull," and then the baron realized it was no dream. He stared and he stared and suddenly he burst into a thunderous laughter, which woke up the whole house. Windows were thrown open and from the cottage, dressed only in their shirts, the boys came running to see what was going on.

Calmly as a horse the elk walked wherever Hoss Peter steered it. Peter rode around the house while the baron, the baroness, the young ladies and the maids were hanging out of the windows calling, "Did you ever see anything like it! Hoss Peter riding the Konga bull!"

But after Peter had ridden around the house he steered the elk towards the two boys in their shirts, standing there with their mouths open. Behind them was the same pond into which they had pushed Hoss Peter. And before they had time to close their mouths the Konga bull took first one then the other on its horns and with a splash threw them into the water.

"Blupp—ohmyohmy, we are drowning, blupp!" they screamed.

At this the baron laughed until he cried. "In that pond a six year old child can touch bottom if he stands on tiptoes," he cried.

Ashamed and wet, with their hair full of weeds, the boys crawled up on the other side and sneaked away. But the baron and all the others laughed until they were almost sick.

When finally they were able to stop the baron said, "Now, what was it you wanted for this feat, Peter?"

"The Chinese lemon-apple trees," said Peter.

"Oh, shame on you!" said the baron. "The lemon-apple trees are my pride and the apple of my eye. But since I promised them to you before witnesses, you'll have to take them if you can manage it."

"Not much left of them," said Peter. "I took them in advance. The Konga bull ate them up."

And then he told how everything had happened, leaving nothing out. The baron groaned, for he thought it a bit hard that his beloved trees had become elk food. But Peter said, "It was lucky for you, baron, that I didn't take you up when you wanted to promise me the whole Dragesholm."

"What's that he says?" asked the baroness. "Were you going to promise Hoss Peter the whole estate?"

"Yes, it wasn't far from it," said the baron. "Who would believe he ever would ride such a horse? And now I actually ought to take out my elk rifle. But it will have to be, for never have I shot a creature which can be ridden. But as for you, Hoss Peter, ride off with the Konga bull as far as the road goes, for we don't want it here. And when you come back we shall see if we can't find something instead of Dragesholm for you."

But Peter said he had got all he wanted, and the elk bull was no longer vicious. It was he himself who had steered it towards the boys to repay them for the last time. But the baron wouldn't dream of having the elk staying in the neighborhood, doing damage to the forest and the crop.

"Now you ride off with it, far away from South Ridge," he said. "That's my last word, or else I shall have to get my gun after all."

"If the elk has to go, Hoss Peter will no longer be seen on the Ridge either," said Peter.

And then he rode away from Dragesholm on the elk. There were many who saw him as he rode off, and many met him on the road, who told about it later on. He rode very slowly, so they said.

The baron could not believe that Peter was serious, so he kept waiting and waiting, but the boy never came back. Where he went with the elk nobody seemed to know. A lot of people guessed he had gone to Halland Ridge, for it was rumored that a giant elk had been seen up there. Some said the Konga bull had appeared up at Kopparhatten, others had seen it at Rävahallen. And once an old soldier said that a boy, riding an elk, had come to the colonel on Bonnarps heath, and asked if they might both go into war service, but the colonel had said no. Not many people believed that story, though.

And the only thing left nowadays, of the boy and the elk, is an old saying, "Well, here I am with the Konga bull, said Hoss Peter."

"That one, at least, you couldn't call a girl story, Pelle-Göran," said Kaja, when Ola Gädda had finished the story.

"No, it was just like a boy's story, a real boy's story," said Pelle-Göran enthusiastically. "Thank you, thank you, nice Ola Gädda."

"And now you have had three stories instead of one," said grandmother.

"Grandfather's was the best one," said Ellen.

Ola Gädda did not just smile then, he laughed out loud.

"Well, look out now, Ola, so you don't spoil that girl," said grandmother. "Don't forget there are other grandchildren on Klövatorp."

"Ye'll see to it, Stig, that I don't forget," said Ola Gädda.

"I sure will," said Stig.

"And now you'll all have to go to bed," said grandmother.

"I'll just get myself a sausage sandwich first," said Folke, "for you know, I promised Kaja that."

"I really think I shall have to lock the pantry," said grandmother, yawning behind her knitting.

"Good night then, and thanks for today," said Ola Gädda, reluctantly walking off.

"Oh, isn't he nice, my grandfather!" said Ellen.

"You go to sleep now," said Stig. And then he, too, said good-bye and left.

Pelle-Göran was so sleepy he almost fell asleep on the attic stairs.

Kaja had to pull him up, and take off his clothes and shoes.

15

Ignaberga Cave

How fast a summer goes!

Both the bilberry picking and the raspberry picking were over long ago. The blackberries were just about finished and the lingonberries were turning red on the cheek turned towards the light. The noise of the threshing machine had stopped at Stubba Farm.

No longer did Stig live in the harness room. Both he and Ola Gädda had moved home to Klövatorp.

It was now settled that Kaja should remain at Stubba Farm. When she heard it she threw her arms around grandmother and cried for pure joy. "Oh, grandmother, you must never die from me!" Grandmother and Folke were just as happy as she, even though Folke went on teasing her now and then. Kaja sang and chirped all day long, and no longer did she cry in her bed when she thought Pelle-Göran had gone to sleep as she had done many a night before.

Tigerpaw and Rosenose were almost half-grown cats

now, helping their mother catch rats in the barn. The chickens were busy laying eggs and Lubbe was still so afraid of the door to the chicken coop, that if a fox had dared to show himself there, he might have allowed it to go free. But as luck would have it, no fox appeared. And if he should happen to come, there was always Amelie to sound the alarm.

At the end of the berry picking time Kaja started school. One day she came home and said she had heard the school children teasing Ellen from Klövatorp during recess, and give her the old nickname.

"I think you ought to look after Ellen a little and be extra nice to her," said grandmother. "Show them that you like her, then perhaps, they might do the same."

During the first recess the next day Kaja took Ellen's arm and walked around the schoolyard with her, eagerly chatting and whispering about the snake bite and Ola Gädda, the big eel and the stories they had heard together. The other children couldn't get over their surprise that Kaja wanted to be with such a little one. "If you only knew how much fun she is," said Kaja, "and what a nice time we had with her and Stig this summer."

And now, wherever the two girls went they had a tail of children after them. They all wanted to know about the fun they had had. When they found out that Ellen had been bitten by a snake, she immediately became of more interest to them, especially when she pulled off her stocking and showed them her two little scars. And when they were told about the coin Ola Gädda had given her, one of the bigger girls said that Ola Gädda certainly wouldn't have done that

if she were a thief. So Kaja told them that the old man had been very angry when he heard that they used to call her that ugly name. And she said that he had moved home to Klövatorp again. By and by the silly talk about the children from Klövatorp died down, and one day when Kaja came out for recess, two little girls from Ellen's class had taken her between them and walked arm in arm with her. The only one who still, once in a while, would call her a nasty name was tall William Nilsson. But one day after school Stig gave him a good thrashing, and after taking that medicine, William Nilsson, too, kept quiet.

Kaja told all about it when she came home. She was

afraid that grandmother might be upset because Stig had been fighting. But grandmother only said, "Well, it might be that a boy like William Nilsson won't be taught manners for less. And I'll say he has been asking for it for a long time."

Pelle-Göran would have liked to go to school, too. He hardly knew what to do with himself since he didn't have anybody to play with until late in the afternoon. Perhaps he had never really appreciated Kaja enough when she was always at hand.

From Stockholm came happy news. Mamma had come home from hospital. She would still have to rest a while before she would be able to take care of a child and a house again. So Pelle-Göran would have to stay with grandmother a few more weeks. But Mamma was well and that was the main thing. In a few weeks he would see her. Not pale and tired in a hospital bed, but well and happy as before and at home!

The days grew shorter, the evenings darker. The hazel nuts in the glen were changing from light green to light brown. And during the nut picking time guests arrived at the farm. It was grandmother's sister Paula and her husband. The children called them aunt and uncle since Folke did. Uncle Hakan was a minister in a parish close to the border of Smaland. He was writing a book on old Skanish country churches and their ministers through the ages. And he had come to South Ridge to take a good look at Kageröd's and Stenestad's churches. He talked to the minister, read church books, took notes and photographs.

Grandmother and Dela were happy to be able to talk over old childhood memories with Aunt Paula, while they helped one another canning vegetables and picking nuts. Every evening it went like this, "Do you remember?" and "Do you remember that time, though?" Kaja and Pelle-Göran listened. It was so strange to think that these three once had been wild and unruly little girls, up to all kinds of mischief.

Once grandmother had talked them into going down to the brook at twelve o'clock at night on a Thursday, to throw a stone in the water. She had said that if they called out: *"Fairy of the brook and sea, Give the wonder gift to me!"* they would see a white, transparent creature rise out of the water to give them a great treasure. But when Paula and Dela, with trembling voices read the verse, grandmother was lying behind a stone whipping the water violently with a big leafy branch. The girls were frightened out of their wits, and rushed home crying they had seen the Brook horse himself. They had taken the branch to be the mane of the Brook horse, the flying mane, of which they had so often heard.

"Well, I don't think we were very good little girls," said grandmother. "And do you remember that time we young people went on a trip to the cave at Ignaberga and Nils Andersson played ghost?"

"Oh yes, and how frightened we were!" said Dela and Paula.

"A cave!" said Kaja. "I have just read a terribly exciting

book from Folke's book case about a boy and a girl who were lost in a cave."

"Tom Sawyer," nodded Folke. "So, you found that one."

"Can't we go to that cave where grandmother was?" asked Pelle-Göran longingly.

Folke said that Ignaberga was not on South Ridge but away down near Hässleholm.

"Oh, why didn't we go there when we went to Hässleholm?" asked Pelle-Göran. "I have never seen a cave."

"I haven't either," said Kaja.

"I was in the old Ignaberga church two years ago collecting material," said the minister thoughtfully. "But I need a little more, and I have no photographs either. Why shouldn't I take a trip there now, while I am here. I think I will call my colleague in Ignaberga parish and ask if it will be all right for me to come after the service on Sunday."

Kaja and Pelle-Göran looked at one another. They didn't feel that they knew Uncle Hakan well enough to ask him if they might go along. But they couldn't help jumping up and down with eagerness on their chairs. Folke noticed it and winked at them.

"Suppose we all take a trip to Ignaberga," he said.

Grandmother, Dela and Paula said, that as far as they were concerned, they were too old for caves. They would rather sit home in peace and talk over olden times while "the kettle hummed," as Dela called it when the coffee began to simmer in the pot. So it was decided that the minister and Folke should go and take the children with them.

"If only the weather won't be bad," said grandmother doubtfully, looking out through the window where the fall rain came down.

"That won't matter, it is dry down in the cave," said Folke. "But speaking about rain, and since Kaja happened to mention old Tom Sawyer, do you remember, mother, the time it rained only on one side of the house?"

Grandmother burst out laughing.

"I should say I do. Yes, that time it was Hans who was up to things, the rascal."

"My Pappa?" wondered Pelle-Göran.

"Yes, he was the one. He was up to all sorts of tricks."

Pelle-Göran was amazed. Although this really wasn't any stranger than that grandmother herself had been up to mischief.

And then he heard about it.

"Well, as you know, Hans was fond of reading even as a child," said Folke. "And one Saturday he had gotten hold of that book, *Tom Sawyer*. Father brought it when he was in Ängelholm to visit the doctor. Hans was so crazy about the book, that he lay in bed reading at night, until father came in and blew out the light. Now we had been told that we were going to church on Sunday morning, if it didn't rain. Hans woke up early and began reading. It was a little cloudy, but it didn't rain. Then Hans got the idea, that Torsten, Erik and I might go and fill the big fire engine at the pond, and then we could spray water on the window of father's bedroom, so that he would think it was raining. And that's what we did. I held the hose and Erik pumped

and Torsten added water with a pail. And all the time Hans lay there, reading for all he was worth. We kept on for quite a while, before we were discovered.

Grandmother laughed.

"Yes," she said. "Father was still in bed, listening to the rain, but finally he came out to me in the kitchen, saying, "Can you make out how it can be raining only on one side of the house and not on the other?" "It's raining?" I said. "I have just been out to feed the animals, and it wasn't raining then." He laughed and said, "Come and you'll see the rain-makers." He pulled me over to the kitchen window, and there we saw how the children were carrying on, all three dressed only in their night shirts. But they had forgotten that there was another window on the other side of father's bedroom. And so they had to go to church after all. But would you believe it, Hans took that book along, and tried to hide it under the hymnbook in the church. But then father took away the book and he didn't get it back for a whole week, no matter how much he begged. You see, father was strict and wanted his boys to obey. And you say, Folke, that was the book about the cave? I had forgotten that."

"But I will never forget it," said Folke. "Hans told us the whole story. He had promised us that before we made the rain. And as soon as I learned to read, I read it by myself. And since then I have read it several times."

"Tell us about that cave," begged Pelle-Göran.

But Folke had no time for it, for one of the cows was about to calve and Folke had to go out to the barn. In the evening after they had gone to bed Kaja told Pelle-Göran that the book was about a whole lot of funny things, and also some rather frightening ones, but the most exciting part was about a boy, called Tom, and a girl, called Becky, who were lost in a cave and almost starved to death, and weren't found for three days.

Then Kaja and Pelle-Göran agreed that they should take both food and flashlight along when they went to the cave at Ignaberga. You'd never know when it might come in handy.

Sunday began with nice weather. They packed a lot of zwiebacks and a bottle of lingonberry juice in Kaja's small suitcase. When they were ready to go they found Lubbe sitting in the car, as he sometimes did. He liked to ride in a car. Kaja pleaded for him and so he was allowed to go with them.

Dela had made a red jacket for Kaja, and on the trip to Ignaberga she wore it for the first time. When Folke saw it he rolled his eyes in enthusiasm.

"You are almost too grand for our simple company," he said. "The only thing lacking is a flower in your buttonhole."

And he took a sprig from one of grandmother's tomato plants and held it out to her. On it were two small tomatoes and Kaja immediately ate them. But to tease Folke she ran upstairs after the old cloth rose and fastened it on her lapel. And there it stayed when they left despite the face Folke made.

"When I get back I'll write to Gertrud and tell her all about the cave," she said, "and I know she'll be glad to hear that her rose was with us all the time."

"You really look terrible," said Folke. "Can't you see that the color clashes with the color of your nice jacket?"

"I think it is nice," said Kaja stubbornly, ruffling her rose which by this time looked quite droopy.

The minister laughed.

"Let her alone, she looks sweet anyway," he said.

Kaja looked at him, and thought he was awfully nice.

"Too bad that you are not a bachelor and a jungle doctor," she said, "otherwise you might have married me."

"Why a jungle doctor?" asked the minister.

"Oh, I read about one in a magazine. He was so wonderful. He helped the natives when they were sick and saved their children from dying of croup, and pulled the thorns from the paw of a jaguar. And everyone loved him and his wife Myra. She was very lovely. She had black hair and eyes as blue as violets and a slender figure. And she helped him with all the operations and the natives just loved her and called her "The white angel."

"Did you hear that!" said Folke. "Now I understand. The jungle doctor is only secondary. Kaja wants to be an angel! That's it."

"Aren't we soon at the cave?" asked Pelle-Göran.

"Not for a long time," said Folke. "But in there lies Dragesholm, you remember, where Hoss Peter was a stable boy."

And Folke turned off to the left so they could see the beautiful estate with the little bridge and the ponds surrounding the manor like a moat. They tried to guess into which pond the elk might have pushed the jealous boys. But they couldn't see anything which might look like Chinese lemon-apple trees.

"I'm afraid they never recovered after all those branches had been broken off," said Folke. "They must have died, I think."

Then they drove along the Klöva Brook and over West Sönnarslöv towards Klippan. There it began to rain, and in pouring, splashing rain they drove through Perstorp and Tyringe towards Hässleholm. But after Hässleholm they weren't far off.

Uncle Hakan's friend, dressed in raincoat, was waiting at the old church in Ignaberga. Uncle Hakan went off. The

178

cave was quite near, so Folke drove over there and parked the car in the parking place.

"Dogs aren't allowed in churches or in caves, so you'll have to stay in the car, old Lubbe," he said. "You had better take the opportunity. Stretch out on the back seat and make yourself comfortable now nobody's looking."

On the slope in front of the path leading down to the cave stood a little group of people with umbrellas over their heads, waiting for their turn to have a look at the remarkable place.

"I have been down in the cave twice," said Folke. "And even if I do think it is great that we have just as fine caves here in Sweden as those Tom Sawyer wandered around in over in America, I think I would rather go and keep Uncle Hakan company. Here you have money for the tickets. Go along with those who go down the next time. If it is raining when you come up, you can go and sit in the car. Otherwise you can come to the church and find us."

Then he left. It was still raining a little. The children crept in under the umbrella held by a friendly old gentleman who felt sorry for Kaja's new jacket.

There was nothing remarkable about the entrance to the cave. It was just like an ordinary cellar door, made from boards and fastened with a padlock. But inside they glimpsed a staircase leading straight down into the ground. It looked eerie and exciting.

"Here they come," somebody said.

And out of the darkness below, ten, twelve tourists emerged, led by a lady with a lantern. They climbed up

into the light and the rain, and those who had been waiting would now have their turn going underground.

Kaja held Pelle-Göran's hand very firmly. In the other hand she carried the bag with the zwiebacks and the lingonberry juice. The children were the last ones. The lady with the lantern went ahead. She was the mistress of the farm on whose property the cave was. While they were climbing down, wandering in along the winding passages and through the larger pillar-decorated rooms, she was telling what was known about the cave.

It was not a natural cave. It was an old limestone quarry. As early as the year one thousand the work had begun in the quarry, and it had continued until about seventy years ago. Workers had dug down to a depth of twenty yards, and there they had cut out limestone in such a way, that it had formed passages and great halls. Pillars of stone had been left standing so the roof would not fall in. The men had done the actual digging, and the women had carried out the broken limestone on stretchers, she said.

The light from the lantern flickered and darted around the roughly cut walls of the limestone cave, and stole into the dark vaulted passages on the sides, so low, that one would have to crawl on all fours if one wanted to examine them further. It was shining on the powerful pillars, some of them so beautifully cut that they might have stood in a church. It made flickering shadow patterns on the ceiling which some places looked like an arch high above, and other places almost touched the heads of the people walking under it.

"To the right here we have unexplored areas where the ceiling has fallen down, and the possibility of cave-ins is so great that nobody is allowed there," said the lady with the lantern. "This one we call the Great Hall. Isn't it splendid with all its columns and the high ceiling. We are almost right below the highway now. If we kept completely still and a car were driving along up there, we might hear it, even though there are more than twenty yards of soil in between."

Pelle-Göran was busy turning on and off his flashlight, and peeking into every hole and side passage they were passing. He only heard half of what the tourists asked and the answers the caretaker gave. It was warm and dry inside the cave and he would have liked to stop to explore it thoroughly and see where all the passages led. He thought the others were in too much of a hurry. But Kaja pulled him along and said they had better not stay too far behind.

Finally they had been all around and walked up towards the entrance again. As they came out they saw other tourists standing there, waiting their turn. It was raining harder now, and Kaja and Pelle-Göran dashed for the car. Lubbe began to whine and to lick them, he was so happy not to be left alone any longer.

Kaja opened the suitcase and took out the zwiebacks and the bottle with lingonberry juice. For now that they were out of the cave, there was no need of saving the food any more. But just as she was about to take a bite of grandmother's delicious zwiebacks, she cried in alarm, "The rose! I have lost Gertrud's rose. Where can it be?"

They searched the car, but it wasn't there. Leaving the zwiebacks and the lingonberry juice, they hurried out into the rain searching all the way to the cave. But nowhere did they see any big candy-pink rose.

"I must have lost it inside the cave," said Kaja. "Oh, if I only could find it. Gertrud will be awfully sorry when she hears I have lost it."

"We'll have to go in again and look for it," said Pelle-Göran, happy that he might get a closer look at those mysterious side passages.

"But we have no money left," said Kaja. "You know, it costs twenty-five öre for children to go in."

182

"Then we'll have to go to the church, and ask Folke for more money," said Pelle-Göran.

But Kaja didn't think that Folke would give them any money to find that poor rose he disliked so much. He would probably say it was fine she got rid of it.

"Look!" cried Pelle-Göran. "The door is open, and nobody is there. We can go in alone and have a look for the rose. We have got my flashlight, you know."

Kaja said that nobody was supposed to go inside the cave except when the lady with the lantern was along. But as she was saying it, she drew closer to the entrance, and Pelle-Göran followed.

"I simply have to find that rose," said Kaja stepping in through the door. "Give me your flashlight, please! The others must be far down into the cave, I can't hear a sound."

Hand in hand they walked down, carefully searching the ground with the flashlight. But no rose did they find. They hurried ahead, trying to remember which hall they had seen, and through which passages they had been before.

"This is it," said Pelle-Göran. "I remember that stone over there, because I thought it looked like the nose of an old man."

After a while Kaja said uncertainly, "But, have we really been here before? I can't remember that the roof was so low."

They went around one column, and across a corridor, and then they knew where they were. There was the opening into the Great Hall of which the lady had been so proud.

"Asch, it's easy enough to find your way here," bragged
Pelle-Göran. But a few minutes later he wasn't quite so
cocksure. For then the light from the flashlight grew more
and more faint.

"The battery is giving out!" said Kaja frightened.
"Come, let's run back as fast as we can before it goes dead."

But that was easier said than done. They didn't even find
the Great Hall, just one little strange cave after the other.
The flashlight was shining fainter and fainter until it all of a
sudden went out. Kaja shook it in despair, but it didn't do
any good. There they stood in complete darkness, not
knowing in which direction they ought to be walking to

get to the opening. Groping along the walls, they carefully felt their way with one foot at a time, so they would not fall into some hole.

"Kaja," squeaked Pelle-Göran, "have we lost our way just like Tom and Becky?"

"You can't get lost in such a little cave," said Kaja as bravely as she could. "Didn't you hear the lady say, it was only two hundred yards long and one hundred and ten yards wide?"

"That's a lot," said Pelle-Göran.

"Oh no, the cave in *Tom Sawyer* was many many times bigger. Don't worry, we'll soon be out, you'll see."

Cautiously they shuffled forward a few more steps.

"And it doesn't matter if we don't find the way out," said Kaja. "For the lady is somewhere around here with the others, and sooner or later they'll be coming by here, and then we can follow them, you know."

"Yes, but I don't like it to be so dark," objected Pelle-Göran.

A little impatiently Kaja said it was because of that silly flashlight.

"We should have taken some candles like Tom and Becky," she said.

"But you told me they had to stay there for three days and pretty nearly starved to death," said Pelle-Göran. "Oh, how hungry I am! And we left the zwiebacks in the car."

"Oh stop it," said Kaja crossly, because now she too was uneasy. "You can't be so very hungry, we ate just before we left!"

185

And she pulled him along with her.

"Suppose we get in where we aren't supposed to be, because the ceiling might fall down on us!" said Pelle-Göran.

Kaja stopped suddenly and caught her breath.

"Sh-h! What was that?" she whispered.

Now Pelle-Göran heard it too. A pattering of soft paws, a sniffing . . .

What could it be? A person? But it didn't sound like one. An animal? What kind of an animal could it be that lived in caves deep down in the ground. Some terrible monster, maybe.

"A dragon," thought Pelle-Göran.

The pattering came closer. It was coming faster now.

Kaja's hand trembled in his. Pelle-Göran was just about to let out a terrified scream, when the creature jumped at him, suppressing his cry, barking, yelping, licking, jumping . . .

"Lubbe," sniffed Kaja, and then she began to laugh. "Oh, darling little Lubbe, it's only you. How did you get out? Pelle-Göran, you forgot to slam the car door after you."

Pelle-Göran had fallen down when the big dog threw himself at him. He was lying on the ground tumbling around with Lubbe, who eagerly continued to lick his face and his ears. He threw his arms around Lubbe's neck, he was so happy. All the safety of Stubba Farm was here with old Lubbe. There was no need to cry any more.

"Hold on to him, Pelle-Göran," said Kaja. "Lubbe will get us out. He'll show us the way. Don't let go of him."

They walked on each side of the dog, holding on to his

collar. Lubbe, of course, was just as blind as they in the darkness, but he had his good nose.

"Folke!" said Kaja. "Master Folke! Go to master Folke!"

The dog panted and pulled, almost strangling himself with the collar. But without stumbling and without making the mistake of walking straight into a wall, the children managed to hang on. And after a while they clearly felt that the passage before them began to rise like a hill.

"Oh, Pelle-Göran, we are on our way up," said Kaja happily.

"Yes, wasn't it lucky that I forgot to slam the car door?" said Pelle-Göran.

"Yes, of course, but oh, how am I going to get my rose?"

Pelle-Göran thought it felt like climbing around in a black velvet bag. The darkness didn't seem so terrible any longer, now when he felt the warm, thick fur against his hand and heard the eager panting of the dog.

And here was the last steep hill, and then they were up.

But what was this? Had they lost their way after all? It was just as dark here as down in the cave.

Kaja cried out. It was a pitiful, defeated little cry.

"Pelle-Göran! The door is locked. Here it is, feel it! They have gone away and locked us in!"

She shook the door and threw herself against it, pounding it with her fists, and Pelle-Göran did the same. They called, but there was no answer. All they heard was the rain pouring down outside. It had a desolate sound.

"Folke! Uncle Hakan! Mrs. Caretaker! Let us out!" screamed Kaja and Pelle-Göran ready to burst into tears.

And Lubbe barked and called, probably the same thing in dog language. But from the outside came suddenly another sound drowning their voices. The thunder had begun to rumble and clap after clap followed. The bright flashes of lightning were shining in to the children through the cracks in the door. Lubbe crept trembling to Kaja and laid his head on her lap. He had always been afraid of thunder.

"I'm sure the lady soon will come down again to show the cave to some other people," said Pelle-Göran. "What do you think she'll say when she sees us? Do you think she'll be mad?"

"I'm afraid there won't be any tourists in weather like this," said Kaja. "Maybe there won't be any before next Sunday."

"Then we'll starve to death," howled Pelle-Göran.

"No, no," said Kaja, throwing her arms around him. "Folke will come and find us, of course."

They called for Folke until they were so hoarse, their voices gave out.

But Folke had already been at the car and had seen that children and dog both had disappeared. He had been at the cave as well but had gone back when he saw the locked door. Then he had returned to the church, for he thought perhaps the children might have gone there, taking another way. But neither Uncle Hakan nor his friend had seen a glimpse of them.

Folke walked over to the farm and asked for them. The lady who had been the guide in the cave said that the children had been with her down in the cave, and after that she had seen them running over to the car in the rain. She had taken another group of tourists down, and therefore she hadn't seen where they went after that. And in the cave, by the way, she had picked up the big rose, which the girl must have lost down there and here it was. When she had brought the group up again, there was nobody else wanting to see the cave, so she had locked the door and gone home. On the way home she had seen the open car door, slamming back and forth, and she had closed it so the rain wouldn't get in. After that, she hadn't given it much of a thought. But she would be glad to call the neighbors, and ask if anybody had seen the children and the dog. But when she called, nobody had seen them.

The lady asked Folke to sit down for a while until the worst of the storm had passed. But Folke stood there with the rose in his hand. He was thinking about the half-eaten meal laid out on the front seat of the car, looking as if it had been abandoned in haste. And he was wondering if Lubbe might have run away and the children might have set out after him. In that case the dog would probably run straight home to his dear Amelie.

He said he would drive part of the way home to see if the children might be somewhere along the road. They couldn't have gotten very far.

As he returned to the parking place, he had a faint hope they might be sitting in the car, waiting for him. But the car was still empty. He drove to the old church and told Uncle Hakan what had happened and what he thought he might do.

"I'll be back soon," he said.

"Wait a moment," said the minister. "Did you say that the girl had lost that monstrous rose thing? Well then, of course she is out looking for it. Where? Down in the cave, since she lost it there. And the boy and the dog must be with her and they have been locked in. We had better go there at once. If they have been locked in they must be frightened to death. Where did you say we might find the key?"

They didn't need to drive all the way to the farm, for they met the lady with the lantern on the way. The same idea had occurred to her.

As they came close to the cave they heard a muffled bark, followed by a long drawn out howling sound.

"Well, thank goodness, there is Lubbe," said Folke.

The rain had stopped and only a few rumblings were heard in the distance. And just as the lady stuck the key in the padlock on the door, the sun peeked out from behind the clouds and made the rain spattered leaves glitter like millions of tiny splinters of looking-glass.

And when Kaja and Pelle-Göran, tear-blinking, screwed up their eyes against the light and the longed for world outside the cave, the candy-pink rose was the first they saw. It hung wet and drooping from Folke's buttonhole.

16

The Cork Pillow

The herring peddler used to come to Stubba Farm once a week with his fish: fresh herring, salt herring, smoked herring, fresh flounders and smoked eel. Pelle-Göran liked to chat with him while grandmother selected her fish. He had asked the herring peddler, just as he had asked everybody else that summer, if he knew where he might get hold of cork for a swimming pillow. And the herring peddler had promised him cork. But he seemed to forget the whole thing. For every time he stopped with his car tooting outside the gate and Pelle-Göran came running out, the peddler scratched himself behind the ear and said, "Oh! It was you, of course, who wanted cork. It's terrible that I should go and forget it. But next time I'll get you a big heap of it, that I promise you."

But the next time he forgot the cork again. And so it happened week after week. The summer passed and Pelle-Göran stopped hoping for any cork pillow. Neither he nor

Kaja went swimming any more, for the water was not very warm any longer. And the autumn sun could not dry them when they came out, the way the summer sun had done.

And now, when it was not so important to have the cork pillow, the herring peddler came and gave him a whole bag full of cork. He had finally remembered his promise.

Pelle-Göran thanked him and ran in to Dela asking her to make that cork pillow she had been promising him for so long.

"Yes, it will be fine for another year, of course," said Dela.

And then she let him choose the material from her scrap bag. He selected a piece which had broad stripes in red and white, like peppermint. And Dela cut it out and began sewing it on the machine, while Pelle-Göran stood beside her and looked at her.

Suddenly the telephone rang and they heard grandmother go to answer it.

Oh my, how happy and surprised she sounded!

"No-o, of all things. Is it really so? And you're already in Värnamo? Well, I'll say what a wonderful surprise! Oh yes, you are so very welcome. Oh, no! No, of course, I'll keep it quiet. When do you think you'll be here? Oh, that's fine. Yes, welcome then and good-bye, good-bye, until then!"

Grandmother appeared in the door. She looked happy and excited, just as if she had received a very fine present. She almost looked a little mischievous, too.

"Dela," she said, "can you come and lend me a hand? We

must do some baking and we shall have to kill some chickens and other things. For in about three hours we are having guests who will stay for the whole week."

"Who are they?" asked Pelle-Göran.

"A couple of very dear friends. Well, you'll soon see," said grandmother, laughing to herself.

Dela was laughing, also. It sounded as if she understood without asking who they were. And Pelle-Göran thought maybe it was a couple of grandmother's and Dela's childhood friends again. That would be fine, for then, perhaps, he might get to hear some stories.

"Can I have a taste when you are baking?" he begged.

"Oh yes, if only you'll promise not to be in our way, for we are very busy," said grandmother.

He walked out to the barn and petted the newest calf and played with Tigerpaw for a while. Then he went to the glen and picked some hazel nuts. He cracked the shells with a stone and ate until he could not hold any more. He saw a hedgehog, which grandmother and Dela called a quilly pig, and he looked at that a while. Then he went in and ate a dab of dough. After that he sat on the steps scraping the bowl which had been filled with cake batter. But then he heard Dela kill chickens in the woodshed, and he went in, because he didn't like to hear the sound of it and think about what it meant. He walked into Dela's room to see if she had had time to do some more work on the cork pillow. And there it was on the table beside the sewing machine. And just look, it was finished. All the corks were already put inside the two square, candy-striped pillows which were fastened to-

gether with a wide piece of cloth. That the pillows were not
sewn together in the middle, well, that was something he
didn't notice.

He was so happy over his cork pillow that he wanted to
try it out right away. The weather was nice. So maybe the
water wouldn't be so cold, even though it was fall. Anyway, he wasn't afraid of a little cold water. Folke still went
swimming in the brook every day. So why shouldn't he be
able to take it.

Pelle-Göran picked up the cork pillow and slung it over
his shoulders. Then he got his swimming trunks and a few
paper boats and hurried down to the brook. He was in such

a hurry that he didn't notice that some of the corks rolled out and fell to the ground.

It did feel a little cool, of course, but not so very cool after all, when he waded out, pulling the cork pillow after him. And it was a wonderful feeling, later on, when he stretched out on his stomach across it, and he felt the two candy striped pillows actually keep him afloat. He really hadn't dared to hope that it would happen. He set his small paper boats afloat and paddled after them.

"I'm swimming," he thought. "Hurrah, I'm swimming. These are just the kind of strokes that Folke and Kaja take. I can do it just as well as they." And he pretended that there was not a bit of cheating in his swimming.

At first he stayed in shallow and safe water inside the stones, as he had been told. But then he became bolder. He pushed the boats out between two stones and followed in their wake. There was nothing to it. He was floating like a duck. It didn't make any difference whether it was shallow water or deep water. Of course, he had heard that where the water lilies grew, or the brook lilies, as grandmother called them, it was very deep and terribly dangerous to go, for there a cow had once gone down and drowned. But the way he was swimming, he couldn't sink.

"Hi there, you water lilies! Hi there, you silly old mud! I don't worry about you, for I am swimming on my cork pillow, that's what I'm doing."

He was going to swim all the way over to the place where Dela used to rinse the yarn she had dyed. Folke had said it

was very deep there. Too bad nobody could see how good he was. Kaja would be surprised when she heard about it.

But . . . what was the matter with the cork pillow? It didn't float so well any longer. It seemed to grow heavier and heavier, and one of the candy-striped pillows had become much thinner. In fact, both of them. But one was worse than the other. It sank a little below the surface and his body went down with it. Maybe there weren't two hundred corks after all, even though Dela had said she was sure there were more.

He felt scared and wanted to go ashore. But the flat stone on which Dela used to kneel when she rinsed the yarn was still some distance away. What were those little things floating all around him? Corks? From where did they come? Was the pillow falling apart?

And now, now it didn't want to hold him up any longer. His head went under, he got water in his nose. Splashing wildly he came up again, screaming, yelling for help, then he went under again . . . cluck, cluck, the water closed above his head. Strangely green, the sun shimmered through the water. He couldn't hear anything more.

Then all became dark as he sank down to the bottom.

When Pelle-Göran woke up from that terrible darkness and that choking feeling, he was lying face down on the grass near the shore. He felt cold and sort of numb. A piece of nutshell cut into his cheek. His nose and his throat were smarting, his head ached all over and his chest felt as if he had swallowed a grater. There was a bubbling sound humming in his ears. And it was so hard to breathe, he wanted to cry. If only he could have managed to get out a cry. And somebody was working with his arms, pressing his back hard and steady, and in a hoarse voice counting, "One, two, three, four, five . . ."

He couldn't understand where he was and how he had gotten there. He just felt more and more that he was terribly ill. When he with much effort opened his eyes he saw a face close to his. And if it hadn't been such a silly idea, he almost could have imagined that it was Mamma's face he saw. He closed his eyes again. Then he heard somebody cry out.

"He moved! He opened his eyes! Oh, Hans, he is alive! Pelle-Göran, dear, can you hear me?"

All he could think of was that the thing that sounded like Mamma's voice must be some kind of a dream, so he didn't try to answer.

"Can you still go on, Hans? Don't you want me to take over?" said another voice. And he was sure he knew that one. It must be Folke's.

197

But the first, hoarse voice, stubbornly and monotonously kept on, mumbling those numbers. And it sounded just as when he counted corks and never reached two hundred. The voice only got to five, and perhaps it didn't know how to count any further, for then it started over again.

"One, two . . ."

"No, six, seven," whispered Pelle-Göran, and then he got the hiccups.

"He is coming to! Darling, don't be afraid!" sniffed the Mamma voice. "That's fine. You just cough now, and get up all that terrible water!"

That hoarse voice stopped counting and nobody pressed him on the back any longer. He lifted his head and tried to turn around. Someone put an arm under him, holding him and helped him to sit up. And then he saw them all. Mamma! It really was she. Pappa! He was the one who had sounded so strange and hoarse. Grandmother in a blue checkered apron. Folke. Dela with blood spattered apron and chicken feathers in her hair.

Mamma cried and laughed at the same time and grandmother dried off a big tear that had run down her nose. Then he began to remember. But it was such a terrible thing to remember, so he didn't want to recall it. And he didn't want to cry, so he didn't look at them. But he did look at Dela for she was smiling all over her face now.

"Look," he said shivering. "Dela has got feathers in her hair!"

Suddenly they began to shout with laughter all of them

and they all wanted to hug him. Folke pinched his toes and started rubbing them.

"You little rascal, you sure did scare us," he said.

But Mamma took him up in her lap and with a sigh he cuddled up to her as close as he could. Folke pulled off his jacket and wrapped it around him. And Dela picked up Pappa's wet shirt from the ground and wrung it out. Then Pelle-Göran saw that Pappa only had on a pair of soaking wet pants.

"Why are you so wet, Pappa?" he asked.

"Pappa jumped in and pulled you out, you see," said Mamma, picking off the nutshell which stuck to his cheek.

"Was I drowning?" he asked.

And then he leaned forward and vomited on the grass.

"You certainly did," said grandmother. "And now it will be best to get you in, where it is warm. You are almost blue with cold."

Pappa carried him. Mamma walked beside him and held his hand all the way up to the farm. He was trembling and shivering with cold, he felt terrible and his chest was hurting, too. But he didn't care about all that. For some strange reason he felt that everything was wonderful after all.

"I don't want to drown any more," he said.

"No, you had better not," said Pappa.

"How did you find me? Did you hear me scream?"

"Yes, I was close by. As soon as we got here I went down the glen to look for you, for grandmother thought you might be there picking nuts."

"Lucky you got hold of me, Pappa!"

"I should say so," said Pappa.

"Oh, how glad I am you came," he said

"So am I," said Pappa.

"It was that silly cork pillow," he tried to explain.

"Next summer I shall teach you to swim, then you won't need any cork pillow," said Pappa.

"Fine," said Pelle-Göran, coughing up some more water.

And then they were home. At the front steps stood a car, a little blue car. It was quite dusty, but one could see it was very new.

"Oh, such a nice car. Did the guests already come?"

"Of course," said grandmother. "I thought you had noticed them."

Pelle-Göran stared.

"Do you mean Pappa and Mamma, grandmother?"

Grandmother nodded.

"Yes, this is our car," said Pappa. "Mamma's and yours and mine. We own it together, the three of us. And in a week we shall go home to Stockholm in it."

"Oh-oh-oh!" said Pelle-Göran.

But though he wanted to go and sit in the car right away, they carried him in to bed.

There they wrapped him in a lot of blankets and rubbed him until he felt warm. Then they gave him some kind of a powder which tasted bad and hot milk with honey which tasted good. After that they asked if there was anything more he wanted. He whispered, "Tigerpaw."

And just imagine, after a little while grandmother herself came, bringing his own dear little cat to his bed. Grandmother who never wanted the cats inside the house, and especially not in the bed!

Tigerpaw promenaded around the bed thoroughly examining it. Then he nestled up to Pelle-Göran's armpit, rolled up there and began to purr, "Urr-urr-urr."

Pelle-Göran looked happily and sleepily at those standing around his bed.

"Listen," he said. "My cat sounds like a car."

He was about to fall asleep. But he struggled against it, he didn't quite want to sleep yet.

"Mamma," he said, "are you all right now?"

"Completely well," nodded Mamma.

"Doesn't it hurt at all?"

Mamma assured him that she didn't have the least pain any longer. That seemed to satisfy him.

"Grandmother," he whispered.

"Yes, my little laddie," said grandmother, ever so gently and lovingly.

"Well, then we'll soon have to bake a spettecake."

"We'll bake two of them," said grandmother.

And with that grandmother's and Mamma's and Pappa's and Dela's and Folke's faces seemed to float together into one bright blur. He fell asleep and slept for a long, long time.

17

Good-bye Old Stubba Farm

The last week on Stubba Farm went all together too fast for Pelle-Göran. He had hardly time to show Pappa and Mamma all the places he had enjoyed and all the animals he had fed and played with before it was time to go home.

But one thing he did have time for, anyway. He helped grandmother bake the spettecake which the doctor was going to have. He helped her with both the beating and the turning. Grandmother, of course, was the one who did most of the beating for she was used to it and had strong arms. And there seemed no end to the time you had to whip when it came to spettecake.

Grandmother took out the iron and rolled paper around the roller which was thicker at one end than at the other. Then she greased it with butter. After that she poured the batter into a pitcher, and began carefully to pour it in rings over the roller, while Pelle-Göran cranked it around and around.

"We'll make the cake along the whole iron, so it will be quite tall, don't you think?" she asked.

"Of course," said Pelle-Göran, cranking and cranking, while grandmother poured the batter, and the spettecake slowly baked in the heat from the beechwood fire.

It took a long time, a terribly long time. And sometimes

his arms became tired. Then Mamma would crank until he could do it again. And grandmother filled the pitcher again and again, and the shiny, yellow batter of eggs and sugar and potato flour stuck to the roler, layer upon layer, while the cake grew bigger and bigger.

When the batter was used up and the cake finally finished, grandmother carefully pulled it off the iron and placed it upright on the table. My, how tall it was!

"Well, if your doctor isn't satisfied with a cake as well turned as this one, he will be very hard to satisfy in this world," she said.

After that grandmother and Mamma helped one another making one more spettecake, and that one they had for coffee the last afternoon. But grandmother wrapped the doctor's cake in paper, put it in a box and tied it up into a big package. Then they put it in the back of the car beside the cases with jars of jam and bottles of juice and a big basket full of nuts which they were taking home to Stockholm.

The next day, early in the morning came time to say good-bye. Kaja was going to ride along with them and get off at the school.

It was hard to part from everything at Stubba Farm and all the people there, grandmother, and Folke, and Dela, and from Lubbe and Amelie and Julius and the calves. But perhaps the hardest thing was to leave Tigerpaw. Grandmother said it wasn't good for cats to live in a big city. And she herself needed Tigerpaw. From the way Tigerpaw had been behaving it looked as if they never would have a better hunter at Stubba Farm. Kaja promised to look after him and said she would write to tell him how Tigerpaw was getting along and what he was doing. "You'll have to come back next summer and see how much he has grown," said grandmother.

Without being told, Pelle-Göran hugged grandmother and said of course he would come back, oh yes!

And after they had said good-bye to people and animals several times they drove out through the gate, while grandmother and Dela and Folke stood waving and waving. The last Pelle-Göran saw of Stubba Farm's inhabitants this time, was Lubbe who stole out through the gate and followed the car a little way down the road, until Amelie's wild quacking called him back again.

At the school they stopped to let Kaja out of the car. Pelle-Göran very much wanted to give her a hug, too. But there were so many children standing and looking at them that he just could not. He only shook her hand and said, "Bye."

"Bye, Pelle-Göran," said Kaja. "It's too bad you have to leave us. Come back again soon, very soon."

"You'll have to come and visit us in Stockholm, Kaja," said Mamma.

"Oh no," said Kaja, sounding almost frightened. "You'll have to come here instead, for I'll never leave Stubba Farm any more."

At that moment the school bell rang. Slowly Kaja walked in backwards, waving all the time.

"Such a nice girl," said Mamma.

"Very nice," said Pappa.

"And doesn't she look cute in that red jacket?" said Pelle-Göran, as proud as if he had made it himself.

And then for a moment, he forgot Kaja and grandmother and everything except this unbelievably wonderful thing, that he was sitting here with Pappa and Mamma in a little car which was their own and that they were going home together all the way to Stockholm.

The beech trees had already taken on their fall colors, and now and then a leaf slowly drifted to the ground in the morning breeze.

"Well, soon it will be winter again," said Mamma.

"And now we are driving down from South Ridge," said Pappa, sighing a little.

"But isn't it a good thing we have this car?" said Pelle-Göran. "Now we can drive back and forth to South Ridge all the time."

18

The Doctor and the Spettecake

Mamma went with Pelle-Göran to the doctor's office but she did not go in with him. She just talked with the nurse a little and stayed in the waiting room while Pelle-Göran was shown in with his big package.

"How do you do," said Pelle-Göran bowing. Then he put his big package on the floor in front of the doctor.

"Hi there," said the doctor.

"Well, here I am," said Pelle-Göran.

"Well, well, what is this I see? If it isn't Pelle, or whatever you called yourself!" said the doctor. "It was you who went to your grandmother, I remember. I almost didn't recognize you. You have grown a lot. And you look fine, too. Well, it isn't so bad to go to Skane once in a while, is it?"

"I want to thank you so terribly much for making my Mamma well," said Pelle-Göran.

"Oh well, it was only what I promised," said the doctor.

"And here I have brought you something you like very

208

much," said Pelle-Göran, moving the package still closer to the doctor's chair.

"Thank you," said the doctor. "And what in the world can it be?"

"Guess," said Pelle-Göran.

"You couldn't possibly have gone and bought a flower pot with such a big flower, could you?" said the doctor.

"Wrong!" said Pelle-Göran. "Guess again."

"Hm," said the doctor, thinking hard. "Let me see. It looks like some kind of tower. A lighthouse, perhaps?"

"Wrong again," laughed Pelle-Göran.

The doctor put his hand up to his chin as if he were in deep thought.

"If it hadn't been so big, I would have guessed a spette-cake," he finally said. "But you just don't find spettecakes that big."

"Oh sure, if you have a terribly big iron and make them as big as the whole iron," said Pelle-Göran eagerly. "Take off the string and the paper, and you'll see it is a spettecake!"

"Really?" said the doctor.

With a pair of scissors he cut the string and pulled off the paper and part of the carton, so the spettecake became visible in all its glory. Then he just stood there staring at it.

"You Pelle, or whatever you call yourself," he said seriously. "This is the biggest and finest spettecake I have seen in all my life. I am wondering, do you think it tastes as good as it looks?"

"Go on and taste it," said Pelle-Göran. "It's your very own spettecake."

"I can hardly believe it," said the doctor.

And then from a glass cupboard behind his desk, he took out a shiny little knife.

"Where do you think we should dig in?" he asked.

Pelle-Göran said that grandmother used to cut out doors and windows. And then he pointed to where they might make a fine door, and where they could open a window. So the doctor cut out first a big door, then a window.

"Grandmother poured the batter over the iron and I turned the crank," explained Pelle Göran while the doctor was cutting.

"Then it's only fair that you taste your own work," said the doctor.

And he held out the piece from the door to Pelle-Göran and took the piece from the window for himself.

"Good," he said, munching happily. "Delicious! Simply the best spettecake I have ever tasted. And I am a real spette-cake expert, I can tell you. Thank you Pelle, or whatever you call yourself!"

"You're welcome!" said Pelle-Göran politely.

For that was what grandmother used to say when people praised her food.

"Oh my, we have spilled crumbs on the fine carpet!" he said a little later. "Won't she be angry, the one who let me in?"

The doctor laughed.

"Maybe," he said. "But look here, we won't take any notice. What about another bite?"

"Mm," said Pelle-Göran.

So they each had another bite.

And if they haven't stopped by now, they may still be sitting there, eating spettecake.